TOM

Daren King was born in Harlow, Essex. He has
published two previous novels, *Boxy an Star*,
which was shortlisted for the 1999 *Guardian*
First Book Award, and *Jim Giraffe*. His website
address is www.darenking.co.uk.

ALSO BY DAREN KING

Boxy an Star
Jim Giraffe

DAREN KING

Tom Boler

VINTAGE BOOKS

London

Published by Vintage 2006

2 4 6 8 10 9 7 5 3 1

First published in Great Britain in 2005 by
Jonathan Cape

Vintage
Random House, 20 Vauxhall Bridge Road,
London SW1V 2SA

Random House Australia (Pty) Limited
20 Alfred Street, Milsons Point, Sydney,
New South Wales 2061, Australia

Random House New Zealand Limited
18 Poland Road, Glenfield, Auckland 10, New Zealand

Random House (Pty) Limited
Isle of Houghton, Corner of Boundary Road & Carse O'Gowrie,
Houghton, 2198, South Africa

The Random House Group Limited Reg. No. 954009
www.randomhouse.co.uk/vintage

A CIP catalogue record for this book
is available from the British Library

ISBN 9780099445159 (from Jan 2007)
ISBN 0099445158

Papers used by Random House are natural,
recyclable products made from wood grown in
sustainable forests. The manufacturing processes
conform to the environmental regulations of the
country of origin

Printed and bound in Great Britain by
Bookmarque Ltd, Croydon, Surrey

Contents

Terry Telly

Me an Terry are watchin telly. It aint a normal telly it is Terry Telly. He aint even watchin it he is it. He is Terry Telly he is tellin me stuff sayin: 'Welcome to a world of fun.'

Me smilin. It is a world of fun.

Terry Telly says: 'I hope you enjoy the show.'

Me smilin.

Terry Telly says: 'Whats your name.'

Me thinkin. Puttin my finger on my chin.

'Go and ask your mum. Find your mum and ask her your name.'

Me gettin off the chair. Runnin on the carpet goin in kitchen. Goin an see my mum. Ask her it. Mum sittin up the table writin on a bit of paper. Not even writin on it lookin at it shuttin her eyes. 'Mum,' I say. 'Whats my name.'

Mum lookin down at me sayin: 'Tom.'

Me runnin in other room on the carpet doin my best run.

It is a best one. Doin it goin in front room. Climbin gettin up on it it is a arm chair the same one what I sat on what I got down offof. Sittin on it sayin: 'Tom.'

'Hello Tom.' Terry Telly says: 'My name is Terry Telly. That is two names. Have you got two names.'

Me noddin.

'What is your second name Tom.'

Me thinkin. Puttin my finger on my chin movin it touchin my mouth.

Terry Telly says: 'Ask your mum.'

Me gettin off the chair climbin down offof it. Runnin on the carpet doin that best one runnin in kitchen ask my mum. 'Mum,' I say holdin on her dress touchin it is blue. 'Mum what is my name. My other one.'

Mum shakin her head.

Me holdin her dress sayin: 'Mum. Mum tell me. What is my name my other one.'

Mum lookin down at me sayin: 'Boler.'

Boler. Me smilin noddin knowin it. Runnin in the other room. Climbin on the chair what I jus got offof. Tellin it to Terry Telly sayin: 'Boler.'

'Put it all together.' Terry Telly says: 'And what have you got.'

Me thinkin. Puttin my finger on my mouth puttin it in. It is that much thinkin.

Terry Telly says: 'Ask your mum.'

Not again. Me gettin off the chair fallin offof it a bit it holdin on my tee shirt pullin it up showin my tummy. Runnin in the kitchen. 'Mum. What have I got.'

Mum shakin her head.

'Mum what have I got puttin it together.'

Mum says: 'Your name is Tom Boler. Youre nine years old. And youre in my hair.'

2

Tom Boler. Run in front room. 'Tom Boler,' I say tellin it to Terry Telly.

'Good morning Tom Boler.' Terry Telly says: 'We are playing a game.'

Me noddin. Playin it. A game.

'Are you sitting comfortably.'

Me sittin on the carpet on my legs foldin em sittin on em. Sittin comfably.

'Then we will begin.' Terry Telly makin a pictures of a lady drinkin a drink it is orange it is squash orange. Terry Telly says: 'Everything has a name. But have you ever wondered where names come from.'

No. I aint.

'This lady is drinking orange squash. You drink orange squash too. But have you ever wondered. Where orange squash comes from.'

Me shakin head.

Terry Telly showin pictures showin em on the screen. It is a factory where they make em makin oranges. 'This is an orange squash factory. This man is putting oranges in to a machine. The machine squashes the oranges.' The machine squashin a oranges doin it like he says. It got big elbows what are metal special made. They doin movin down on em squashin em makin a squash orange. 'That is how orange squash is made.' Terry Telly says: 'And how orange squash gets its name. Say it after me. Orange squash.'

Me sayin it after Terry Telly sayin: 'Squash orange.'

'That is how orange squash gets its name. Now.' Terry Telly says: 'How did you get your name.'

Me shruggin. Not knowin.

'Ask your mum how you got your name.'

Me gettin up un bendin my legs. Goin in the kitchen. 'Mum. How did I get my name.'

'I told you. I keep tellin you.'

'Mum how did I get my name.'

'I married your dad.' Mum says: 'Your dads name is Boler. We had you an you got it.'

'What about the Tom bit. Where did that bit.'

'I gave you it. I told you. Its a joke.'

Me goin in front room not runnin doin it a bit of a walk an a bit of a run. An a bit of fallin over. Careful doin runnin when you are memberin. You will forget it it fallin out your head.

Terry Telly says: 'How did you get your name.'

'I. Um.' I forgot.

'Everything has a name.' Terry Telly says: 'Whats my name.'

'Terry Telly,' I say smilin.

'Ask your mum.'

'I know it,' I say. 'It is Terry Telly. Same as what it is.'

'Welcome to a world of learning.' Terry Telly says: 'Find your mum and ask her my name.'

Me frownin. Walkin. Askin my mum.

'Im busy.'

Me lookin at her lookin at a bit of paper. 'Mum what are you writin.'

Mum pickin it up screwin it up sayin: 'Tom go an watch telly.'

Me goin in front room. Lookin at telly. Terry Telly. Turnin it off.

This is my room. It is got my name on it on the door on a bit of paper. It says. Well. It dont say nothin. I done it wrong.

This is my book. It is got animals in it in cartoon. It is

my best book what I got. I done colourin in. In it an on it an. On the wall. Mum told me off.

This is my fishes. It is made of paper cut out hung up. Made it at school take it home hung it up. Dad hung it up he is big he is on a oil rig.

This is my jim jams. It is got hole in it where I put my head an hole in it where I put my hands an hole in it where I put my feet an hole in it where I put my widdle doin piddle.

This is Poll Tax Clown my bear. He is my friend my best one.

Thing is with Saturday is. Aint normal day it is Saturday. Day of no school same as Sunday an day of watchin telly same as every day. Go in front room turnin on telly sayin: 'Mum. Can I watch telly.'

'No.' Mum says: 'Go an get ready for school.'

'It is Saturday.'

'Its Monday.' Mum says: 'Go to school.'

Me makin a face. Aint even Monday it is Saturday. Aint even mornin it is after a noon. Aint even makin a face it is finish. 'Mum. Why are you wearin that one for.'

'What one.'

'That one. That blue one.'

'What. This.' Mum touchin her dress showin me it. 'Theyre all blue. I always wear blue.'

'But what you wearin that one for your best one.'

'Its a spring dress. Its spring.' Mum touchin it it is spring showin her skin. 'Tom get up them stairs an get your things on for school.'

Me goin up stairs doin as Mummy says. Gettin ready for school. It is Monday same as Mummy says. I am gettin ready for school gettin my school trouser out the chester draws puttin em on. Put shirt on school one short sleeve one. Get my bag out got stuff in it school stuff. It is: Pee ee kit. Readin book. Pencil case shape like space ship. Same as space ship shape like pencil case flyin in space but. Other way round.

Run down stairs. Go in front room. Mum watchin telly it aint even turned on sayin: 'Aint you gone yet.'

Me shakin head.

'You better get goin then aint you.'

Me noddin. Goin in front door bit at bottom of stairs. Jus when I am turnin handle openin front door it openin some one comin in. It is milk man bringin milk. 'Sorry milk man,' I say. 'Aint got time for no milk. It aint even mornin.'

'Thats alright.' Milk man laughin comin in sayin: 'Wheres your mum.'

School is fun it is. Makin stuff. Doin stuff. Cuttin things out. Colourin things in. Playin a game with a other boys an a girls. Knicker chase. Widdle chase. Piggy in a middle. Nose chase. That aint even a game I made it up.

It is fun school is but it aint fun on a Monday on a Saturday on a own. Sittin in play ground not even playin. Aint even got no one to play with. Aint even no one ere. Other boys an girls aint ere. It is Saturday in their house it—

'Bole.'

'Oi Boler.'

'Boler.'

It is that lot. That lot of big boys from Big School. Little end of it they aint proper big boys leavin school gettin a job gettin groan up. Bigger than me though. I am at big end of Little School they are at little end of Big School. They are called Groin an Thick Ear an Hair Cut. That one what is called Groin is kickin a foot ball kickin it at me sayin: 'Fancy a kick around.'

Hair Cut says: 'Yeah fancy a kick around.'

Thick Ear says: 'Yeah.'

Me noddin. Fancyin it. A kick around. Kickin it. A ball.

Groin says: 'What you doin ere any way Boler. Its Saturday.'

'I am at school,' I say. 'It is Saturday on a Monday. A school day. I am at school.'

Groin gettin the ball kickin it at me but not right at me right near me kickin it round me runnin round me stoppin it sayin: 'What you come ere on your own for. We jus come ere for a kick around. Good place for a kick around.'

Hair Cut says: 'Some one go in goal.' He is tall got funny hair cut shaved up this end an out the other. 'Thick Ear you go in goal.'

Thick Ear dont say nothin. He dont hardly never say nothin he dont.

Hair Cut says: 'Go on. Get in goal.'

It is a goal painted on a concrete we are on it a concrete. Thick Ear lookin at it. A goal.

Groin says: 'Let Bole go in goal. I wanna kick it at his head.'

Me makin a face. Dont want to.

'Go on.' Groin says: 'Go in goal. Its a new game whats come out. Head Ball. Kick it at your head.'

Me shruggin. Puttin my school bag in a bushes. Goin in goal.

Groin an Thick Ear an Hair Cut runnin round kickin it doin a tackle an kickin it at my head. It missin me movin out the way.

Groin runnin gettin the ball pickin it up shoutin: 'Bole dont keep movin.'

Alright. I am not keep movin. Jus standin ere not even

movin. It is Head Ball a game what you play with big boys kickin it at your head. Groin kickin the—

Ouch.

It hit my head.

'Goal.' Groin shoutin it runnin round he is scored a goal he is a champion shoutin: 'Goal.'

'That was fun,' I say. 'I am goin home.'

'No you aint.' Hair Cut comin up to me touchin up his hair sayin: 'Ninety minutes each end. Come on Thick Ear you have a go. Oi Groin. Let Thick Ear have a go.'

Groin puttin the ball on a line in front of goal me standin in it.

Thick Ear runnin up to it stickin his finger in his ear cleanin his brain out. Gettin ready. Kickin.

Missed.

Groin gettin the ball runnin after it gettin it it rollin in the bushes by the door what is can teen door sausage an chips aint even nice. 'Whose go is it.'

Hair Cut puttin hand in air. Then. In his hair.

Groin noddin settin ball on line sayin: 'Go on then. Kick it at his head.'

Hair Cut checkin his hair in mirror what aint even proper mirror it is sun shinin on window of class room. Gettin it right. Turnin. Lookin at ball. Walkin. Not runnin dont want to mess up his hair. Gettin ready. Kickin.

Missed.

Groin grinnin goin gettin ball shoutin: 'Oi watch me. The champion.' Not even puttin it on line jus runnin with it kickin it bootin it me watchin it it gettin bigger an—

Ouch.

Where am I. Where—

I am on a concrete layin ere lookin up at the sky it spinnin—

It is a lovely day it is spring. It is a lovely day for a kick around. Playin foot ball with a big boys three of em what—

Hang on. They aint big boys they are little boys the same one. It is a boy what is in my class. My eyes goin funny makin it look like three boys what was big boys but aint no more but it. It is a boy what is in my class.

'Where did them big boys go.'

The boy comin over not sayin nothin. He dont never say nothin he aint even from round ere he is from a other country he is called Marco Meccano he is a His Panic. Marco Meccano gettin down on his knees pickin things up little things what are round me shinin like stars what fell out my head when I got hit.

It is in London but it aint London in Marco Meccanos house it is His Panic. It is his house what he lives in with Mister Meccano an Misses Meccano. Mister Meccano pickin me up like pickin up a olive holdin it in his finger an thumb squeezin it like in a advert. Pickin me up holdin me up. He is a big man got a big tummy got a big belt goin round it like a road goin round it an cars. Pickin me up holdin me up sayin: 'Hola hola hola.'

Me noddin.

Mister Meccano puttin me down givin me to Misses Meccano it is takin it in a turn. Misses Meccano pickin me up throwin me up in a air at a ceiling hittin my head catchin me sayin: 'Hola. My sweet little English onion. Hola.'

Me noddin. Want to get down.

Misses Meccano puttin me down. Me sortin my self out tuckin my shirt in coverin up my tum. It is a tiny tum same as Mister Meccanos thumb.

Marco Meccano smilin at me sayin: 'Persaroso. Excusa.'

Me shruggin. Dont know what he is on about.

Marco Meccano pointin at a ceiling what I jus hit on my head sayin: 'Arriba.'

I am Tom. I have got a con fuse.

Marco Meccano holdin on my short sleeve shirt sleeve pullin me up a stairs goin up stairs. Gettin half way up turnin corner sayin: 'Arriba.'

Me noddin. Goin up stairs. Aint a normal stairs it is a His Panic stairs. It aint got carpet on it is wood got gaps in fallin thru. Turnin corner goin up stairs up in to topper part of Marco Meccanos house.

Marco Meccano standin at top turnin round sayin: 'Alcoba. Dormitorio.'

Me goin in Marco Meccanos bed room followin him in. It is like a normal bed room but His Panic. Me goin in it sayin: 'Your dad is fat.'

Marco Meccano shruggin.

Me makin a face makin it fat. Blowin up my cheeks. Holdin out my arms makin it like a shape of a fat dad what he has got.

Marco Meccano smilin noddin pointin down stairs sayin: 'Si si si. Obeso.'

'My dad is better than your dad,' I say. 'My dad is on a oil rig sailin a seven seas. He is a proper dad. Not like your dad.'

Marco Meccano sittin on bed.

Me sittin down on a side of bed tellin him like tellin a story sayin: 'Some dads are rubbish an some dads are a best dad. My dad is a best dad. He is on a oil rig. Drillin oil in a oil drill.'

Marco Meccano noddin. Frownin.

'Your room aint rubbish though,' I say cheerin him up. 'It is a good one.'

Marco Meccano shruggin.

'Is that your bear.'

Marco Meccano lookin at his bear pickin it up smilin sayin: 'Oso. Tasa Idiota.'

'Is that what his name is,' I say pointin at it. 'What it is called.'

Marco Meccano noddin grinnin sayin: 'Tasa Idiota.' Givin it a kiss.

Funny name for a bear. 'What else you got.' Me lookin round his room. Lookin what he got.

Marco Meccano gettin off his bed sayin: 'Globo. Mundo globo.'

Me shakin head sayin: 'No no no. Not globo. Globe.' Makin a shape of it in my mouth. Shape of it an shape of word of it. 'Globe.' It is a globe a map of world a round one spinnin round. Me spinnin it findin in a middle of a sea pointin at where it is blue sayin: 'Look. That is where my dad is. On a oil rig.'

Marco Meccano makin a face sayin: 'Globo.'

'You carnt talk proper,' I say sayin it nice. Then. Hearin a noise. Sayin: 'Whats that noise.'

Marco Meccano makin a face. Holdin his nose. Doin it like it is a smell but it aint.

It aint a smell it is a noise comin from out side window. Me goin to window curtain liftin it lookin out it. It is a lot of noisy girls playin in garden makin noises. It is sunny in garden an girls play in it lappin it up.

'Hermana amistades.' Marco Meccano holdin his nose pointin at girls sayin: 'Apestoso hermana.'

'Shall we play out.'

Marco Meccano shakin his head. He aint playin out.

I am playin out. Runnin down stairs runnin round house

11

lookin for door of garden runnin out of way of Mister an Misses Meccano dont want to get that hug. Mister an Misses Meccano lookin at me laughin it is funny a joke. It aint a joke it is girls playin in garden bein pretty.

Now I am got out ere they aint even out ere. It is jus me out ere on a own. An a voice sayin: 'Aceituna.' Me lookin up. It is Marco Meccano got bed room window open hangin out it eatin a olive. It is a olive tree growin up out side of house. Marco Meccano pickin olive offof olive tree eatin it spittin it at me it is a pip.

Me lookin at tree. It is a big tree it is a big garden got a lot of trees in it. Best tree is olive tree growin olive. Olive is a fruit what taste of olive oil. Branches growin in Marco Meccanos window growin in his mouth olives growin in his tummy him eatin em spittin pips at me it is pip boy machine gun.

Peep out of be hind tree hidin be hind it. Lookin up at Marco Meccano lookin out of window lookin for me carnt see me I am hidin.

Where is that girls.

Peep out of be hind tree. Look up at Marco Meccano but. He is gone.

Where is that girls. They are gone. Carnt see em an carnt even hear em an. Carnt smell em they dont even smell they are pretty. Lookin at girls is like lookin at flowers an sun an ice cream an lookin at your mum. I am goin to look for em. Where are they. Me lookin for em walkin cross the grass feelin cross. They are hidin like me hidin from Marco Meccano but he was spittin pip I aint spittin pip I aint even got it. Carnt spit what I aint got. Where are they gone. There is a lot of trees what I can hide be hind them girls

hidin be hind em lookin at me laughin at me. Me lookin
for em lookin for the girls what—

I have found somethin.

Me gettin down have a look. It is a girl thing what a girl
wears on a arm wrist lookin pretty it is a bracelet. It is pink
an it is white like petals an shells an pretty things all in a
row on a bit of string. Me lookin at it. Thinkin. Puttin my
finger on my chin. What I am thinkin is. It aint what it is
it is where it is. It is on a little path what comes offof big
path what I am on. Me walkin down it that little path.
Lookin for them girls what—

I have found somethin.

It is a doll what girls play with doin girl things with. Pick
it up have a look. What a pretty eyes it has got. All a better
to look at me with. It lookin at me not even seein me it is a
doll a toy what aint even real. I am real I am thinkin. Puttin
my finger on my chin movin it touchin my mouth. What I
am thinkin is. What if I follow things what them girls have
dropped. Things what they are playin with. Playin it so busy
they drop it. I am walkin down path lookin for things what—

I have found somethin.

It is. A pair of knick knocks. That is the name of girl
pants. Same as boy pants but. Pretty. They have got flowers
on it an silly frilly lastic. Me pickin it up. Thinkin. Puttin
my finger on my mouth puttin it in. It is that much thinkin.
What I am thinkin is. I aint thinkin about knick knocks it
is rude thinkin about em your mum tellin you off. What I
am thinkin is. Where there is knick knocks. There is girls.
An where there is girls. That is. That is where they are.

Me lookin at where I am thinkin. It is. A wood shed
shack. Walk quiet touchin it that wood. Careful touchin it
you get splinter cryin go an see your mum. Your mum gettin

metal tweezer tweezin splinter gettin it out. Plant it in garden it growin makin a tree. Chop it down chop it up make it a wood shed shack.

I aint touchin it that wood shed shack. I am climbin tree what is next to be side it growin up over it climbin up in topper part of it. Then. Climbin down gettin on roof of wood shed shack. Doin it quiet. Layin. On it. Peerin. Over it. A edge.

They are in it. Up side down but. They are in it.

Hmm. Me thinkin.

It aint them what is up side down it is me what is up side down makin em look up side down. They are down side up. Or. What ever it is called. They are in it in wood shed shack sittin talkin. Their voices comin out of it out of window what is broke. One of em talkin loud shoutin sayin: 'What are you going to be when you grow up.'

'Well.' Other girl says: 'Im going to be a great lady from Den Mark. I am going to be. A great Dane.'

'Youre not from Den Mark.' Loud girl says: 'Youre from round here. You carnt be from where youre not from.'

'Im going to go there.' Den Mark girl says: 'And live there. And come back. And be from there.'

'Your mum wont let you.'

'She will.' Den Mark girl says: 'Im going to be older than my mum. When I grow up.'

'You wont. Youll grow up and your mum will grow up.' Loud girl says: 'You wont ever be older than your mum.'

'My gran dad is.'

'Hes a man.' Loud girl shoutin loud out of loud mouth what she has got givin it all shes got. 'Men are always older. Two years older. Dont you know anything.'

'I know lots of things.'

'Like what.'

14

Den Mark girl sittin up straight givin it to her straight straight from the horses mouth sayin: 'Im going to be queen.'

'You wont be queen.' Loud mouth girl says: 'Youre going to be poor. A pheasant.'

One of other girls two of em lookin at loud mouth girl sayin: 'Whats a pheasant.'

'A farmer.' Loud mouth girl lookin at Den Mark girl sayin: 'And thats what youre going to be.'

Den Mark girl shakin her head. 'I will be queen. And I will have you hanged by the neck. Until your eye balls turn in to diamonds. And Im going to spend them. And buy a beautiful dress. And marry. An edible bachelor.'

'You wont marry an edible bachelor.' Loud mouth girl says: 'Youre going to be ugly. The edible bachelor will be sick. Youll be left on the shelf. And you will marry. A kermit.'

The one of them other ones lookin at loud mouth girl sayin: 'Whats a kermit.'

'A lonely old man. Who lives alone. And smells.'

Den Mark girl shakin her head. 'He wont smell. Im going to wash him. And polish his bald nose. And we will make. A baby.'

'You will make a baby.' Loud mouth girl says: 'But it will come out dead. The nurse will throw it in the dust bin. And eat it.'

The other one the same one lookin at loud mouth girl sayin: 'Whats that.'

'What. A dust bin.'

The girl pointin at somethin. At the window. At my head.

'O that.' Loud mouth girl says: 'Thats a boy. Shall we get him.'

They aint goin to get me. I am gettin away runnin away. Did quick way of gettin offof roof of wood shed shack fallin

15

offof it landin on somethin soft landin on my head. Same as in a army on telly. But. Littler. I am little I am Tom Boler I am doin runnin doin my best run.

No time for thinkin when I am doin runnin.

When I done lots of runnin gettin away I sit down get a breath back. My heart doin thumpin in my tummy. Doin it like I am gettin told off but I aint. I am. In the garden. It is big aint it this garden is. Me lookin round it. Carnt see it jus see trees. I am like a army man in army in garden hidin from girls. Girls bein like baddy army goin to get me. They aint though. They are girls I am a man bein manly doin it in a army. Puttin mask mud pack on. Gettin mud mixin it with spit puttin it on my face.

Me scrabblin thru a under growth. Scramblin over humps an bumps. Goin over a top. Duckin an divin. Wrigglin. An gigglin. Then. Not gigglin doin it serious a army.

It is big this garden is. I aint I am little. Gettin littler an littler gettin far away gettin lost. The quiet gettin louder. Trees gettin taller. Animals gettin hairier. Plants gettin spikier. Then. I am got there. A end of a world.

Aint nothin I can do. I am. Givin it up. Walkin. To the girls. Lettin em have it they have won.

It is only a bit of a walk an them girls come out of be hind trees comin to come an get me. That loud mouth girl givin a order sayin: 'Get him.'

Den Mark girl grabbin holdin my wrist sayin: 'What shall we do with him.'

Loud mouth girl thinkin. Then. Noddin sayin: 'In terror gate him.'

'Where.'

'At the gate.'

Girls takin me to garden gate. Den Mark girl holdin my wrist givin it a twist twistin it off. Other girls two of em followin. Loud mouth girl leadin. It is follow a leader. Up the garden path. To the house.

Me lookin up at window. He is there. Pip boy machine gun. He is a boy he is on my side goin to rescue me. Gettin ready firin pip. But. He is full up. Carnt eat olive if he is full up.

Loud mouth girl leadin down side of house down a alley way to garden gate. Openin it. Den Mark girl goin out it shuttin it. Puttin my hands thru it. Holdin my wrists holdin me thru gate.

Out there there is cars. If I was groan up I would go out there an get in a car an drive. Them girls chasin me. Gettin in a girl car it is pink. Me in blue car drivin fast gettin a way. But. I aint. I am a kid I am caught. Den Mark girl holdin my wrist twistin em. Loud mouth girl sittin on gate. Other girl standin watchin. One of em is His Panic. She is sister of Marco Meccano she dont say nothin carnt talk proper. It is her garden it is her friends playin in garden come round playin out.

'Right.' Loud mouth girl says: 'Tell us your name.'

'Tom Boler.'

'Any other names. Made up names.'

'Bole,' I say. 'Please dont beat me up.'

'Girls dont beat boys up Tom. Im going to ask you things. And if you dont answer. And tell me about boys. Im going to wee on you.'

'No.' Me wrigglin doin it a lot but. Carnt get away. Loud mouth girl movin along gate sittin over me. Openin her legs. 'No dont,' I say. 'My mum will tell me off.'

17

'She will tell you off. You wont be allowed out no more. Now.' Loud mouth girl says: 'Tell us about boys. Tell us what they are like.'

'Like girls but. Better.'

'Better.'

'Well.' Me shruggin. Not doin it proper carnt do it proper I am caught. 'Not better but. Bigger.'

'Youre not bigger.'

'I know I aint Im littler. That girl,' I say pointin at girl what is His Panic. Point my finger it is only thing what can point. 'Her brother is in my class. He is a younger brother. An thats why I am littler.'

'So boys arent bigger.'

'Well,' I say. 'Not bigger but. Stronger.'

'Youre not stronger.'

'I am.'

'Prove it.' Loud mouth girl says: 'Prove how strong you are by getting away.'

Den Mark girl says: 'Shall I let him get away.'

'No.' Loud mouth girl says: 'Hes got to try to escape. If he does it if he escapes. It means boys are stronger.'

Den Mark girl noddin. Smilin. Holdin me tight. Twistin. Me strugglin. Makin a strong face. Tryin an get away but. Carnt.

'Now.' Loud mouth girl says: 'Tell us about boys. About what is different about boys. Different than girls.'

Me thinkin. What I am goin to say.

'Quickly.' Loud mouth girl liftin her dress. Over my head I can see her knicks.

'Dont wee on me,' I say cryin. 'Please dont wee on me.'

'I will wee on you.' Loud mouth girl says: 'I had fizzy orange. And. An ice pop. You better say it quick. Or I will wee.'

Me thinkin. What is difrent about boys. Difrent than girls.

What it is. What is difrent. Things what they do what boys do. Foot ball. Pretend you have got a gun. Play fight. Head lock. Eat a bit of mud. That sort of stuff. But. That aint it that aint a thing about em. It is a thing what they do. It is. What I got to say is. A thing what is about em. About boys. What is difrent about em. About boys.

'Quickly.'

Me thinkin. Lookin up at them knicks. Lookin at em. Thinkin. Then. Knowin. Sayin it quick sayin: 'I have got a widdle.'

No one says nothin. Then. Loud mouth girl shuttin her legs sayin: 'Show me.'

'No.'

Loud mouth girl openin legs sayin: 'Ive still got that wee.'

'Alright.' Me cryin. Sniffin. 'I will show you it but. Dont tell my mum. She told me not to show it.'

It is done. I have shown my widdle. Showin it to that girl the loud mouth one. In that wood shed shack. Other girls waitin out side it. Loud mouth girl shuttin door shuttin em out. Tellin me to get it out. Me. Gettin it out. Thinkin: She is goin to laugh at my widdle. But. She didnt even laugh at it jus looked at it thinkin about it an what it is like. She aint got a widdle she aint. I aint looked but. Girls aint got one they have got a hole.

When it is done it is time for Girl Club. Girl Club is a club what is for girls. Aint no boys in it. Jus girls. Even if I want to come in it they wont let me in it. 'Can I come in it,' I say. 'In that Girl Club.'

'No.' Loud mouth girl says: 'Its for girls.'

'O.'

Loud mouth girl shuttin wood door of wood shed shack. They are in it. I aint in it. I am out it. Knockin on door sayin: 'If you let me in it. I will show you my widdle.'

'No.' Loud mouth girl shoutin thru door sayin: 'Ive seen it. Its silly.'

'Can I come in it,' I say. 'An not show you it.'

No one sayin nothin. Nothin even happenin. Only birds singin in trees they are happy. Then. Wood door openin. Loud mouth girl pokin her mouth out. Sayin: 'Wheres your widdle.'

'In my pants.'

'Come in then.'

Me goin in.

Loud mouth girl shuttin door.

'I dont like bein a boy,' I say. 'It is rubbish.'

Then. Jus as she is sayin it. Door openin. Some one runnin in. A girl. Little. Even littler than what I am an I am little. Runnin in. Shoutin: 'Boys smell of poo.'

Loud mouth girl lookin at her. Frownin. Sayin: 'Stacy get out. We arent ready for you yet.'

Stacy makin a face. Frownin. Foldin her arms. Doin it funny foldin em too big. Hidin half her face. Turnin. Gettin out.

'Now where was I.'

'You was lettin me join Girl Club,' I say fibbin. 'Can I join it then.'

Loud mouth girl lookin at other girls. Other girls. Lookin at loud mouth girl. Loud mouth girl. Lookin at me. 'Yes. But only if. You wear a dress.'

Den Mark girl says: 'Margo.' Sayin it to that His Panic girl. 'Go an get Tom a dress. One of your dresses.'

His Panic girl Margo Meccano older sister of Marco Meccano goin an gettin dress. Standin up. Openin wood door. Goin out it shuttin it.

'Am I in it then,' I say gettin excited. 'In that Girl Club.'

'Not quite.' Loud mouth girl says: 'There is a joining up ceremony. We take you to an in chanted garden. At the bottom of the garden. And sing to you. About you. And dance around you. And turn you in to a girl.'

'What about my widdle.'

'We get rid of it.'

'O.'

I am goin to wear a dress I am goin to be a girl in Girl Club. Playin in garden. Gettin married. Talkin about animals cute ones aint they. Drinkin fizzy orange. Eatin a ice pop. Mixin it in my tummy makin lemon ade.

It is a fairy ring in in chanted garden. Girls standin in it. In a ring. Holdin hands. Singin: 'Lily Lane. Lily Lane. Whats your name Lily Lane.'

Me standin in middle. Wearin dress. Lookin down at it. At flower bits an silly frilly bits. Feelin it. What it is like. Feelin silly.

What is it like. It is like. A cake. Me wearin it. A cake.

I am a boy but. I am like a girl. Girls dancin round me singin: 'Lily Lane. Lily Lane. Whats your name Lily Lane.'

'I aint Lily Lane,' I say. 'I am Tom Boler a boy.'

Girls not listenin. Dancin round me. Singin: 'Lily Lane. Lily Lane. Whats your name Lily Lane.'

'Dont,' I say. 'I aint even Lily Lane.'

'Lily Lane. Lily Lane. Whats your name Lily Lane.'

'Dont,' I say runnin pushin past pushin thru girls that circle shoutin doin my best run. It is a boy thing runnin is. Im good at it at doin runnin I am a boy.

*

I am a boy but. I am in a dress. Carnt go home if I am in a dress. Every one laughin at me. Callin me a girl. Sayin I am pretty givin me a kiss. Lookin up my dress at my widdle. Mum tellin me off. Pullin down my pants. Smackin my bum.

That is why I am hidin. In a under growth. Under cover. Like in a army. A girl army a pretty one wearin dress.

Dont even want to be ere. In a garden. On a own. Waitin. Tummy rumblin. Growlin. Like. A animal. Hidin in garden goin to eat me it is hungry.

There is two difrent scared. One scared is scared of scary garden on a own in the dark. Other scared is scared of gettin told off gettin home gettin a smack. That scared of garden makin me walk home. That scared of gettin smack makin me doin it slow keep stoppin. It gettin dark. Me. Gettin lost.

Aint no one can see me. It is dark. Time for nunnights. But. Carnt go nunnights. Aint even at home. Dont even know what way it is. I do know it but. When it is dark it is difrent.

I am got home. Walkin in back door. Turnin light on wavin at it sayin hello. It is how you do it turnin it on it is special it is hi tech.

'Mum.'

Where is she. She aint ere. She aint in the kitchen doin a washin up an she aint in the front room watchin telly. I am in it watchin it turnin it on the telly. Terry Telly. But. It aint Terry Telly it is difrent. It is Terrence Telly for groan ups. Sayin: 'Welcome to a world of responsibility.'

Me makin a face. Dont like it.

'My name is Terrence Telly.' Terrence Telly says: 'Whats your name.'

He aint even talkin to me. I aint even a groan up.

'Whats your name.'

Me lookin round. Aint no one there.

'Whats your name.'

'Tom,' I say shruggin. 'I aint even a groan up.'

'What are you doing up this late.' Terrence Telly says: 'It is past your bed time.'

'Im waitin,' I say. 'When it is bed time. Mum says it is bed time.'

'Where is your mum.'

Me shruggin. Not knowin.

'I know where she is.'

'Where.'

'In bed.'

'O,' I say standin up. 'I am goin to go up there. An have a cuddle.'

Terrence Telly shakin his head it is square. 'Not her own bed. A different bed.'

'What difrent bed.'

'Tom you know that man.'

'What man.'

'The milk man man.'

Me noddin. That man.

'He isnt really a milk man. That man and your mum. Pretend he is a milk man. For a joke.'

Me shruggin. Dont get it.

'Tom do you know what sex is.'

Me shakin head.

Terrence Telly not sayin nothin. Lookin at me. Makin me look at his eyes they are square. Then. Sayin: 'Sex is like kissing but. Worse.'

Me makin a face. Dont like it.

'When he comes round. That man. And your mum. Have sex.'

'They dont,' I say. 'She dont even do it. If she does do it. She does it with my dad.'

'Where is your dad Tom.'

'On a oil rig.'

'Hes not on an oil rig.' Terrence Telly says: 'Hes in prison. On drugs.'

'O. Well,' I say. 'Where ever he is. My mum an dad. Dont even have sex. It is mucky.'

'They do have sex.' Terrence Telly says: 'But not with each other. Your mum has sex with the milk man who isnt really a milk man. And your dad. Has sex. With big hairy men.'

'O.'

'They beat him up and do it while hes asleep.'

Me noddin. Learnin. It is a birds an a bees.

Me goin up stairs. Gettin that dress off. Puttin it in washin basket hidin it pushin it right down. Goin in my room. In the nuddy. Puttin on my jim jams. Puttin my head in hole where I put my head an puttin my hands in hole where I put my hands an puttin my feet in hole where I put my feet. Then. Goin in bath room. Pokin out my widdle. Pokin it out hole where I put my widdle. Doin piddle.

'Mum.'

Where is she. She aint in her room. Even liftin up the blanket she aint in it. She aint under the bed. Aint be hind the curtain.

Me lookin in her war drobe. At her dresses. They are blue but. They are gone.

Uncle Dustman

A dust man is a man what goes round in a dust cart what stink of rubbish. Dust man puttin rubbish in it makin it stink. Gettin rubbish what is in bags what people dont want puttin it out side their house. Dust man puttin it in dust cart drivin off.

I am goin an seein my uncle. He is nice he is. Uncle Dustman his name is. He is called that because he is a dust man.

'Hello Uncle Dustman,' I say to my Uncle Dustman shoutin it thru letter box. 'It is Tom. I have come an see you.'

Me waitin. On door step. Out side Uncle Dustmans house.

Door openin Uncle Dustman openin it sayin: 'Tom mate. Bring your self in mate.' Sayin it it is a sir prize. Aint no one never comes round an sees him. He is a dust man. Aint no one goin to come an see a dust man. 'How you doin then

25

Tom mate hows tricks.' It is a small house it is jus one room got front door in it an back door out it goin out in alley what is toilet. Uncle Dustman shuttin front door sayin: 'Sit your self down mate.'

Me sittin on mattress what Uncle Dustman does sleepin on. When letter comes thru letter box it lands on his head. If you write to him dont do it on Friday it comes on Saturday landin on his head wakin him up. Dont like gettin waked up on a Saturday he dont.

'Been watchin me new video player mate.'

'What.'

'Video player. Old fashion thing it is. They dont make em no more. Got it on me round. Flick your eye balls at this mate.' Uncle Dustman holdin up somethin what he has got sayin: 'Video cassette tape. They dont make em no more. See them. Them two round things.' Pointin at two round things what are in the under neath of the video cassette tape. 'Spools theyre called mate. Flick your eye balls at this bit mate. Like sticky tape but it aint got no glue on it.'

'Whats it got on it then,' I say. 'If it aint got no glue on it.'

'Pictures mate.'

Me takin the video cassette tape lookin at it. Lookin in it. Lookin for pictures but. Carnt see em.

'Too small for the naked eye Tom mate. See that.' Uncle Dustman kickin somethin what is on carpet in front of telly on the carpet. 'Video player. Picked it up on me round. Video cassette tape goes in this slot in the front.' Uncle Dustman postin that video cassette tape in front of video player like post man postin letter thru letter box it landin on Uncle Dustmans head. Video player takin it suckin it in eatin it. Lights come on on front of it.

Then. Nothin happens.

'Whats it do Uncle Dustman.'

'Plays films mate.'

'Wheres the films then,' I say. 'What it plays.'

'Press that try angle button.' Uncle Dustman sayin: 'Bit groan up for you though Tom mate. Adult content. Only got the one. Have to get you some cartoons. See what I can pick up on me round. Right Tom jus poppin out for a pony.' Uncle Dustman puttin his boots on what he has already got on because he is a dust man openin back door goin out in alley doin a poo.

Me waitin. Lookin at telly.

Lookin at it. Thinkin: What if I press it. That button. That try angle one.

Jus when I am goin to press it back door openin Uncle Dustman comin in.

Me sittin down not doin nothin sayin: 'Aint you doin your poo. Your pony.'

'Carnt could I. Bloke out there walkin his dog.' Uncle Dustman pressin button what make tape come out takin it out puttin it in pocket of his jacket what he calls his donkey sayin: 'Adult content mate.'

'I am a adult.'

'Youre a kid Tom mate. If I showed you that film. What would your mum say. Chop my nackers off.'

'She wont chop your nackers off. She wont do nothin. Shes busy.'

'Doin what mate.'

'Doin sex,' I say sayin it quiet. 'With that man.'

'What man.'

'Milk man man. What aint really a milk man. It was on the telly.'

'What you on about.' Uncle Dustman sittin on edge of mattress. 'You mean on that hi tech telly thing you got.'

Me noddin.

'It shouldnt tell you that sort of stuff. Thats groan up stuff.' Uncle Dustman tappin side of video cassette tape sayin: 'Adult content.'

'I watched it in the night time. In the day time it is Terry Telly. In the night. It is Terrence Telly for groan ups.'

'Well when shes finished doin. Doin what shes doin. Thats when she would chop em off.'

'She wont finish.' Me shakin head talkin quiet goin all quiet. 'Shes taken her dresses.'

'What dresses.'

'All of em.'

'Tom mate you aint makin sense Tom mate.'

'In her war drobe,' I say. 'Where theres her dresses. There aint dresses.'

'Well where are they.'

Me takin my envelope out of trouser pocket. Folded up. Un foldin it.

Uncle Dustman not watchin. Standin up openin back door. 'That blokes gone. That bloke with the dog.' Uncle Dustman goin out doin poo.

Me lookin at envelope. On it it says: 'End of tether reached. Please send more tether.' Then. Jus when I am goin to open it. Back door openin Uncle Dustman comin in.

'That bloody dog. Blokes need a pony too you know.'

'Why carnt you do it,' I say. 'Your pony. It is a dog a animal.'

'It aint the dog Tom mate its the dog owner.'

'Doin a pony.'

Uncle Dustman laughin. 'Takin the dog for a pony. You

can tell its doin a pony. The leash goes tight. When the leash goes slack. Its done it its done its pony.'

Me noddin. Learnin. He is clever my Uncle Dustman is. Even if he is a dust man. He is clever. That is why I have come an see him. Show him that envelope. Me showin it him sayin: 'Look.'

'Whats that Tom mate.'

'A envelope.'

'Where you get that from.'

'Kitchen table. Mum wrote it. She left it. When she left.'

'Slung her hook then has she.'

Me noddin.

'When did this happen.'

'Yester day. It is Monday on a Saturday. I went a school. Then. When I got home. She is slung that hook.'

'No one goes to school on a Saturday. Day of rest Tom. And today. Then tomorrow Im back on me round. If I can get the bloody thing workin. Me dust cart. The mechanism. In the back. Compressor. Wont compress. Aint you gonna open it.'

Me lookin. At the envelope. Shakin my head.

Uncle Dustman not watchin. Takin his clobes off. Not ones what he is wearin. Ones what he is worn piled up. Takin em offof somethin what they are piled up on droppin em on carpet. 'Know what this is.' Uncle Dustman tappin it. Tappin what it is. Tellin me what it is. 'Ye olde micro wavy overn.'

'What.'

'Old fashion thing it is. Dont make em no more. Before your internet oven come out. Had to make do with one of these. Cookin a meal could take anythin up to one minute Tom mate.'

Me openin my mouth. 'One minute.'

Uncle Dustman noddin.

'Didnt people get dead.'

'What you on about. Starvation.' Uncle Dustman takin somethin out of pocket of jacket callin it his donkey sayin: 'Talkin of which. You know what this is.'

I do know it. What it is. It is. A fish.

Uncle Dustman wavin it about. It swimmin in air like in a water but. Stinky. 'Got it on me round. You hungry.'

'Is it dinner time.'

Uncle Dustman lookin at his watch. 'As good as. Half past four an a half. Good watch this is. Picked it up on me round. Shows the time in hours an minutes an seconds an half seconds. That way. Even if you dont know if youre comin or goin. You know what day it is.'

'Are we goin to eat that fish.'

'Does a donkey do a pony.' Uncle Dustman puttin fish in micro wavy overn shuttin door. Pressin button turnin it on. Fish spinnin. Me an Uncle Dustman watchin. Uncle Dustman lookin at me sayin: 'You do look hungry Tom.'

'Aint had no break fast.'

'Whys that then Tom mate.'

Me shruggin.

Uncle Dustman pressin button makin a ping makin door open. Puttin finger in. In micro wavy overn. Then. In fish. Pokin. Sayin: 'Still a bit green around the gills.' Shuttin door. Pressin button turnin it on. 'You had your dinner last night though right.'

'I was playin out,' I say. 'Dont get no dinner if you are playin out.'

Uncle Dustman not listenin. Pressin button makin that ping makin door open. Uncle Dustman pokin nose in micro

wavy overn. Then. In fish. Sniffin it puttin in it a bogey.
'Thats done Tom mate that is.' Uncle Dustman turnin round
bendin down. Liftin up mattress pullin plate out sayin: 'Best
family silver. Dont want that goin astray. Flick your eye balls
at that Tom mate.' Uncle Dustman showin me the plate.
Wipin on it his sleeve. Holdin it up. Showin me it. It is a
painting of a donkey. Doin a pony.

'Is it a antique.'

'Kind of.' Uncle Dustman says: 'Its older than you are.
Older than I even. When I was your age.' Uncle Dustman
flappin fish on plate sayin: 'Grab a fork mate an tuck in.'

'Where is it Uncle Dustman.'

'In the pen shoe.'

Me bendin down findin that pen shoe. It is a shoe what
has got pens in it. Not jus pens but. Pens an things what
are like pens. What are like em. Like. Pencils. Scissors. Toe
nail tweezer clippers. An forks. Me grabbin a fork tuckin in.
Standin up. Sayin: 'Shall I get you one Uncle Dustman.'

'No need Tom mate.' Uncle Dustman doin a trick. Movin
plate up side down doin it quick. Fish jumpin in a air it is
alive it is a fish out of water. It aint though. It is a trick. It
landin on Uncle Dustmans face. Uncle Dustman grinnin
under neath it bitin it. 'What you laughin at Tom mate.
Aint you never seen a bloke eat a fish off his face before.'

Me laughin. At that trick.

'A bloke gets lonely.' Uncle Dustman grinnin under neath
it eatin it. 'Thats how they did it in the old days Tom mate.
Before they invented forks.' Uncle Dustman droppin fish on
plate sayin: 'Tuck in.'

I am well lucky I am. Havin that Uncle Dustman. He is a
best uncle what is a dust man what ever I had. I am walkin

home goin home from that Uncle Dustmans house goin an seein my mum. She is comin home she loves me she is my mum.

I am. In the street. Out side my house. Waitin. For my mum. Waitin an waitin an waitin but. She aint come.

Where is she.

It is a hour an a half an a bit an she aint ere. It is after a noon an she aint even ere.

Takes ages doin that sex does. How long it takes. I am goin an ask some one a groan up. Me goin up the road our road knockin on a door on a house reachin up knockin that door knock.

That there. Over there. That is my house.

Me waitin at a door on a house. Door openin. Ginger hair lady openin it lookin out it. Lookin over my head I am little. 'I am down ere,' I say. 'I am little.'

Ginger hair lady lookin down.

'I am come to ask you about it.'

'About what.'

'It. Doin it,' I say sayin it quiet. 'Sex.'

'Not today thank you.'

'Not jus today,' I say lookin up at that lady. 'Every day. Today an yester day an today.'

'Are you windin me up. Youre too young.' Ginger hair lady gettin cross sayin: 'Youll have me locked up.'

'I dont mean doin it. I mean about doin it. How long it takes.'

'You shouldnt even know what it is at your age.' Ginger hair lady says: 'Let alone how long it takes.'

'I do know what it is,' I say. 'It is like kissin but. Worse.'

Ginger hair lady shakin ginger hair head. Shuttin door.

Me lookin at door. Reachin up. Knockin.

Door openin ginger hair lady openin it sayin: 'What.'

'I am askin you,' I say. 'About it.'

'What you wanna know for.'

'My mum is doin it. I am just askin. How long. It is.'

That lady gigglin. 'Youll have to ask your dad that.'

'He is in prison,' I say. 'On a oil rig.'

'It must be bloody long then. If hes doin it with your mum. An hes in the nick.'

'It aint even my dad what is doin it,' I say. 'It is a milk man. What aint even a milk man.'

'You been readin too many saucy post cards.'

Me shakin head.

'Then where did you pick up ideas like that then. House wives an milk men.'

'She said he is a milk man but. When he comes round. She wears that dress that spring one showin her skin.'

'It must be love.'

'No,' I say shakin my head doin it quick stoppin that love. 'She dont love him. She loves me. Shes my mum.'

'Dont mean she loves you. I dont love my mum.'

'Have you got a mum.'

Ginger hair lady pointin at hair what is ginger. That point goin thru it goin up stairs. 'Shes up stairs.'

'How old are you then,' I say. 'If you have got a mum.'

'Dont be so ruddy rude.'

Me frownin. Gettin told off.

'Sorry I dont mean to be crabby but you dont go round askin some one their age. At my age.'

'Im nine.'

'Well Im forty two. Now you see why you dont ask it.'

'How olds your mum then.'

Ginger hair lady lookin up at sky. 'Shes a dino sore. Do you like biscuits.'

Me noddin. I do like em.

Ginger hair lady openin cubberd gettin out it a biscuits. It is ginger nut one. Openin that biscuits holdin em out.

Me takin one bitin it. It is big.

The lady takin one bitin it. It is little.

'They are nice ones aint they.'

The lady noddin. Crunchin. Swallowin it is gone.

Me lookin at my biscuit. 'They are big ones aint they.'

'You wont be wantin a nother one then.'

'I will be wantin a nother one then,' I say. 'I aint had no dinner. I am well hungry I am.'

'Dont your mum feed you.'

'She is gone,' I say. 'She aint comin back. Not when she is doin that sex.'

'Done a bunk then has she.'

Me noddin.

The lady openin the cubberd gettin that biscuits out that same one. Then. Jus when she is gettin it. Stoppin. Turnin. Lookin. At me. Sayin: 'So shes done a bunk then has she.'

Me noddin.

'With a fella.'

Me noddin.

'Dark hair. Chirpy. Dark curly hair.'

Me noddin.

'Thats my ruddy husband.'

'O.'

'My ruddy husband.' Foldin her arms. Shakin her head. 'I knew it I ruddy knew it. You live over the road there Tinas boy.'

Me noddin.

Ginger hair lady puttin ginger nut biscuits on side board doin it cross brokin em. 'Now you know why I been so ruddy crabby.'

'You aint been crabby,' I say smilin. 'Ruddy crabby. You have been nice.'

'My husband dont think so. Else. He wouldnt have run off. Where ever his cock goes he follows.' Ginger hair lady shakin ginger hair like shakin pepper pot makin pepper come out. 'He only popped out for a pack of biscuits.'

Me lookin at the biscuits. I want one.

'Saturday this was.'

'Yeah it was. It was Monday on a Saturday,' I say. 'I went a school. Mum made me go a school. Then. When I come back. She is gone.'

Ginger hair lady openin chair at table sittin down at table. 'Ruddy kill him. Thought hed fallen down an hole. Wondered what had happened. Wish he ruddy well had now. Sorry Tom I dont mean to be crabby.' Ginger hair lady lookin at me lookin crabby. 'It is Tom aint it. Tinas boy.'

Me noddin.

'Im Audrey Laundry. So whats gonna happen to you then.' Audrey Laundry shakin her head sayin: 'You aint got a mum.'

Me smilin. 'It is everythin is alright. I have got a uncle a dust man. Uncle Dustman.'

'An hes gonna look after you then is he.'

Me noddin.

'Well make sure he feeds you.' Audrey Laundry givin me them biscuits sayin: 'Ere look take them biscuits.'

It is time for bed but. Aint no one puttin me in bed. Me sittin on bed. On side of it. Not gettin in it. Not gettin my jim jams on. Not gettin clobes off. Not doin nothin.

'Poll Tax Clown,' I say sayin it to Poll Tax Clown. 'Time for bed Poll Tax Clown.'

Poll Tax Clown not doin nothin. He is a bear carnt do nothin bears carnt.

'Come on Poll Tax Clown,' I say. 'It is time for your bed time.'

Poll Tax Clown not doin nothin. It is rubbish bein a bear is. Bein little an got stuffin in. Gettin told off. Fallin off the bed. Gettin people treddin on.

Me gettin my jim jams out of pillow what they are under. Puttin em on Poll Tax Clown. Or. Puttin Poll Tax Clown in em. He is little he is a bear they are big jim jams for kids. 'Come on then,' I say gettin cross. 'Get in bed.'

Poll Tax Clown not doin nothin.

'Come on,' I say. 'Am I goin to have to smack you. Do you want a story.'

Poll Tax Clown not sayin nothin. Dont want nothin. He is a bear. Dont want nothin they dont. Not even a story. Or. A hug a bear hug.

Me gettin his jim jams offof him gettin my clobes off what I have got on puttin em on that jim jams. Puttin em on. Puttin on the jim jams. Gettin tired gettin in bed.

It is mornin I am waked up.

It is mornin but it aint proper mornin. Aint no mum wakin me up gettin cross gettin the grumps. Sayin: It is time for goin a school do your school work that learnin.

I aint gettin up. Aint even gettin that move on.

What I am thinkin is. If there aint a mum. Makin me get up. Makin me break fast. Makin me go a school. I aint got to go a school.

Then. Jus when I am thinkin it. I heard it a ding of door bell.

Me gettin up gettin dressed. Takin my jim jams off puttin my yester day clobes on doin it wrong. Puttin pants on in side out out side in puttin that trouser on wrong legs in wrong one wrong way round runnin down stairs fallin down em openin front door.

O.

It was goin to be my mum but. It aint.

It is. Uncle Dustman.

Uncle Dustman smilin sayin: 'Mornin Tom mate. Wheres your mum.'

'She is gone doin that slung that hook.'

Uncle Dustman stoppin smilin. 'She still not back.'

Me shakin head.

'Shufty over.' Uncle Dustman pushin me out the way not doin it nasty doin it nice he is nice. Uncle Dustman comin in leavin door open it is spring. 'Tina.' Uncle Dustman sayin my mums name sayin: 'Tina.' Goin up hall lookin in front room lookin in kitchen sayin: 'Tina you there love.'

Me shakin head. She aint there.

'Tina are you up there.'

'She aint there,' I say comin up stairs. 'Her dresses aint there.'

Uncle Dustman goin in mums room. Lookin in war drobe. At dresses. What are blue but. Aint there. 'Buggered off aint she.'

Me noddin.

'He must be some lay that milk man bloke. Doin her so hard she forgets her own son.'

'An me,' I say. 'She forgot me.'

'I said you. Never mind any road.' Uncle Dustman puttin

his hand on my back takin me down stairs sayin: 'You can help us out. Me compression mechanisms broke. Wont compress.'

'How can I help you out Uncle Dustman.'

'You around all day. Hang on can I use your loo.' Uncle Dustman openin back door goin out side sayin: 'Need a pony.'

'The loos up stairs Uncle Dustman.' Me runnin back up stairs showin him. Showin Uncle Dustman where it is. But. He aint there.

Me lookin in loo. Flushin it makin a face.

'Uncle Dustman.' Put seat down stand on it. Openin bath room window. Lookin out. Down. On Uncle Dustman. Standin in garden doin poo. It is a little garden a scruffy one got weeds in. 'The loos up ere Uncle Dustman.'

Uncle Dustman lookin up. 'You around all day.'

Me noddin. He carnt see it he is out in garden I am be hind wobbly window standin on bog loo seat. Shoutin: 'It is Monday a school day but. I aint goin a school. I aint got a mum. I aint got to go a school.'

Uncle Dustman wipin his bum on sting nettle lookin up shoutin: 'Thats handy Harry. Me mechanisms broke. You can help us out.'

Me stretchin up openin cubberd door topper one lookin in cubberd. I am hungry need a break fast. There is a box of that break fast one what I like. It is got a picture of a tiger on it doin smilin. In big smilin writin it says: Anthony Tiger. It is my bestest one it is for kids. Me climbin up on bottom cubberd openin topper one gettin it out that Anthony Tiger. Shakin box hearin it jumpin about.

Look in fridge what is in it. It is. Brussel sprout. It is a veggy table. Get that veggy table put it in rubbish bin it is rubbish. What else. Egg in egg box. Ham meat. Pint of milk. Get out pint of milk shuttin door shuttin in that stink.

Why is it stinky. Everythin is that way. Mums smell nice makin everythin smell nice. When your mum is havin sex it makes everythin stink.

Where is bowl my best one my Bole bowl. It is in sink. Get it out sink turnin on tap wash it. Pour in Anthony Tiger stripy cereal ones in bowl pour in milk. Then. I am jus when I am openin spoon drawer gettin spoon out it is a ding of door bell.

Me runnin in front room goin in front door bit at bottom of stairs. Openin front door. 'Uncle Dustman,' I say sayin it to my Uncle Dustman.

'Shufty over.'

'What is it Uncle Dustman.'

'Rubbish.' Uncle Dustman standin holdin black rubbish bin bags of rubbish. Shuftyin me over pushin me in comin in. 'No sign of your mum then mate.'

Me shakin head.

Uncle Dustman goin up stairs carryin that black rubbish bin bags of rubbish. Goin in Mums room. Me followin. Uncle Dustman openin war drobe door puttin em in war drobe shuttin it shuttin in that stink. 'She wont mind. Only short term.' Uncle Dustman lookin at me smilin sayin: 'Storage mate.'

'I am havin a break fast.'

'Youre a growin lad.' Uncle Dustman goin down stairs sayin: 'You look after your self mate. Back in a bit.' Uncle Dustman goin out sayin: 'Might as well leave it open mate. Back in a bit.'

'Bye Uncle Dustman.'

'Back in a bit.'

Me leavin it open. It is a lovely day it is spring lettin it in. Goin in kitchen sittin up table. Eatin Anthony Tiger tuckin in. It is stripy an orange an got sugar on it an in it. Eatin it. Thinkin: What is that sound. It is sound of some one in hall it is Uncle Dustman. Me goin in hall sayin: 'Is that you Uncle Dustman.'

'Dont mind me Tom mate jus droppin off some stuff.'

'What stuff Uncle Dustman.'

'Refuge.' Uncle Dustman goin up stairs comin down stairs sayin: 'Dont worry Tom mate anythin good you can have first pickins. Mostly jus general house hold waste.'

'What Uncle Dustman.'

'Rubbish. Ere Tom mate flick your eye balls at this.' Uncle Dustman smilin doin a joke. Un doin his donkey jacket liftin up his vest showin me his tummy sayin: 'Whats that remind you of Tom mate.'

Me lookin at it it is hairy.

'Go on Tom mate. Im doin a joke.' Uncle Dustman says: 'Whats it remind you of.'

'Oil,' I say shruggin. 'In a jungle.'

Uncle Dustman frownin. 'O. Never mind any road. You can shut your front door now Im off.'

'What about that rubbish,' I say lookin out front door pointin up stairs. 'That rubbish bin bags of rubbish.'

Uncle Dustman gettin in front of dust cart shoutin: 'All done.' Startin it up. Drivin it off.

Me standin watchin. Watchin that turnin back of dust cart it is empty. Frownin. Shuttin front door. Goin up stairs havin a look. Openin mums bed room door. Havin a look. It is full of rubbish bin bags of rubbish. On the bed an on the floor an rollin out the war drobe veggy tables rollin out round ones.

*

School is borin but. Not goin a school is borin. Aint got nothin to do. Me lookin for somethin to do. Gettin a book. It is called: Things To Make And Do. Sittin up table doin it. Cuttin things out it. Stickin things in it. That sort of stuff. Fun stuff.

In it it says:

HOW TO MAKE A PIGEON
1. Get a roll of toilet roll.
2. Put it in the toilet.
3. Leave it to dry on the radiator.
4. Paint eyes on it.
5. It is hollow and feathery and dry. It is a pigeon.

Me shakin head not even makin it. Turn page thinkin what I am goin to make.

Then. Jus when I am thinkin it. It is ding of door bell. Me runnin in front room goin in front door bit at bottom of stairs. Letter box openin voice comin in sayin: 'Tom darlin its me your mum.'

Me openin front door.

Uncle Dustman laughin sayin: 'Only me Tom mate pullin your leg shufty over.' Uncle Dustman shuftyin me over liftin rubbish bin bags of rubbish liftin em over me carryin em in.

'There aint room in my mums room,' I say. 'You have filled it all up.'

'No worries mate where theres a will theres a way.' Uncle Dustman takin the rubbish bin bags of rubbish up stairs puttin em in bath room. Puttin em in bath an puttin em on bog loo seat. 'Them ones are leakers. Carnt have em gettin mucky on your mums carpet. Your mum. Chop my nackers off.'

'Uncle Dustman,' I say holdin my widdle. 'I need a piddle.'

'You can go in the garden.' Uncle Dustman says: 'Like everyone else.'

I am in garden doin piddle. It is a little garden a scruffy one got weeds in it. Gettin my widdle pointin it at fence doin piddle on it on fence. It goin thru fence goin in next doors garden. Ethnic minority next door neighbour pokin head over fence sayin: 'Whose that pissing on my leg.'

'Sorry mister. I am doin piddle.'

'Well why are you insist on doing it in my garden.'

'I am doin it in my garden,' I say doin it. 'It is goin in your garden it is a accident.'

'Well face the other way.' Ethnic minority next door neighbour gettin cross sayin: 'And who was that taking number two in flower bed earlier this morning.'

'It aint a number two,' I say puttin it away. 'It is a pony.'

'But the flower bed.' Ethnic minority next door neighbour shakin funny shape head.

'It aint flowers it is weeds,' I say lookin at that weeds. 'It is my Uncle Dustman. His mechanisms broke.'

'Then he should see the doctor.'

'He carnt hes busy. Hes a dust man he is collectin that house hold waste.'

'Yes hence the donkey jacket.'

'He is puttin it in my house. That is why. I carnt go a toilet. In my house.'

Ethnic minority next door neighbour scratchin funny thing what is on his head.

'There is rubbish in it. In my house. In the bath room,' I say. 'In the bath an on the bog loo seat.'

'Well why didnt you say so.' Ethnic minority next door

neighbour openin broke bit in fence sayin: 'Come on in and utilise mine.'

'My mum told me not to talk to ethnic minorities.'

'I am London born and brown bread.' Ethnic minority next door neighbour says: 'Just like you.'

Me climbin thru open broke bit in fence.

'Thats it.' Ethnic minority next door neighbour closin broke bit in fence sayin: 'Thats it.'

'You have got a beard.'

Ethnic minority next door neighbour laughin shufflin beard sayin: 'Now how did that get there.'

'It grew on it.'

'I can see we are going to learn a lot from each other.' Ethnic minority next door neighbour bendin down on funny trouser knee holdin hand out an mine an shakin sayin: 'Fatwa Jihad.'

'Tom Boler,' I say shakin.

Fatwa Jihad openin back door goin in. Me goin in followin. Fatwa Jihad walkin up stairs sayin: 'Do you like trains Tom.'

Me shakin head.

'You dont like trains. You dont like to see my train set.' Fatwa Jihad openin bed room door goin in. 'You dont like to see my train set Tom. Runs on authentic steam.'

Followin him in lookin at train set sayin: 'It aint even real.'

'Of course not.' Fatwa Jihad says: 'Its a model train set. What would it be doing fitting in my front bed room if it were a real full size loco motive.'

Me shruggin.

'Any how business before pleasure. The toilet is at the back. The same as your house in fact but in mirror image.' Fatwa Jihad says: 'I shall stoke the engine.'

'Is it a ethnic minority train.'

'No such thing.' Fatwa Jihad says: 'A train is a train. That is the beauty of trains. Theyre trains.'

Me goin in bath room. Get my widdle out point it at ethnic minority toilet. It is a normal toilet same as what we got but. Ethnic minority. A toilet is a bog loo. It is a beauty of it but. Carnt go. 'I carnt go,' I say goin in train set bed room puttin away my widdle. 'I done it in the garden. On your funny trouser.'

'There is nothing funny about my trousers.' Fatwa Jihad says: 'Until you pissed on them. I must change them. You may watch. But dont touch.'

Me watchin. It is a long one a ethnic minority one. Movin makin stuff come out comin out white.

'Its a fine one isnt it Tom.'

Me noddin. It is.

Fatwa Jihad goin out of train set bed room goin in other bed room changin trouser.

I am watchin that train. It is a long one a ethnic minority one. Movin. Makin that noise. Runnin me over cuttin me up.

Fatwa Jihad come runnin in shoutin: 'Tom what in the name. Tom what is it.'

Me not sayin.

'Tom whats going on what happened.'

Me not sayin. Not knowin.

Fatwa Jihad holdin me liftin me up kneelin got my head on his knees doin holdin. 'You are screaming and I rush in and you are all to pieces in the corner. My train set all to pieces.'

Me not sayin nothin. Not knowin. Then. Memberin. 'It runned me over cuttin me up.'

'Tom its a toy toy trains do not run over a boy.'

'I have got a cut.'

'Wheres a cut.' Fatwa Jihad movin my arms checkin em like doctor checkin em. 'Tom where. Wheres a cut where.'

Me lookin at arms. There aint one.

'Tom this is most dramatic and un likely.' Fatwa Jihad sittin up sayin: 'Tom I am very seriously worried. Where is your mother. Let us speak with her.'

'She aint my mother,' I say sittin up. 'She is my mum. An she aint there shes gone away run away doin that done a bunk. I have got a uncle. What I am look after.'

'You mean that you are being looked after by your uncle.'

Me noddin.

'Then we must speak with this uncle. With the utmost urgency.' Fatwa Jihad pickin up his train loco motive sayin: 'The moment I have performed major repairs to my loco motive.'

When you broked somethin. What happens is. You get told off. So. Do runnin off. Then. Carnt get told off.

I have broked it that train set train. Fatwa Jihad not tellin me off but. Not lookin at me lookin cross lookin at train mendin it shakin his head sayin: That boy that boy. Me runnin out of front bed room runnin down stairs runnin out goin out side out in garden.

Where is it that fence bit. That fence bit what open what is broke. Me movin difrent fence bits tryin it.

Carnt do it.

Then. Jus when I am carnt do it. Some one shoutin: 'Tom mate.'

Me lookin up. The look goin over fence up in a air like foot ball big boys kickin it. Lookin up at window what is window goin in my bed room.

'Tom mate.' It is Uncle Dustman lookin out my bed room window shoutin: 'Wondered where youd got to. What you up to. What you doin in next doors garden.'

'I am stuck,' I say shoutin. 'I am in a next doors garden. The next door neighbour. Opened that fence broke bit.'

'Well open it again an come back.'

'I carnt find it,' I say shoutin. 'That broke bit.'

'Climb over.'

'What.'

'Climb over. Put your foot on a flower pot or somethin. An climb over.'

Me climbin over it. Puttin foot on flower pot on flower puttin my foot in it. O. I have broked it. 'I have broked it the flower,' I say shoutin it at Uncle Dustman.

'Dont worry about that jus climb over.'

Me climbin over. Jumpin down a other side in garden in weeds. Goin in house. When I get in it Uncle Dustman is come out my room comin down stairs. 'What you doin Uncle Dustman,' I say sayin it to my Uncle Dustman.

'Droppin off some stuff. Work related.' Uncle Dustman openin front door what is already open goin out in spring blue sky smilin sayin: 'How about givin us a hand.'

Me smilin. Helpin my Uncle Dustman. When I grow up. I am goin to be a dust man. Jus like my Uncle Dustman. 'I am helpin you aint I,' I say sayin it to my Uncle Dustman.

'Thats right Tom mate.'

I am helpin. Goin out side. Carryin the rubbish bin bags of rubbish puttin em in house. Carryin em up stairs puttin em in my bed room.

'Storage mate.' Uncle Dustman pilin em up sayin: 'Only short term. Drive down the depot later have em take a look.' Pilin em up at window makin it dark. 'Keep that window open get some fresh air. Does get stuffy these modern houses.'

'Where am I goin to sleep Uncle Dustman.'

'Why. You tired.' Uncle Dustman says: 'Its the middle of the after noon.'

'Not now,' I say. 'When I am helped you. When it is night time.'

Uncle Dustman scratchin his hair gettin muck on it. 'Hadnt thought of that. Its a mugs game Tom mate. Thinkin is. For mugs.'

Me lookin at my bed at rubbish bin bags of rubbish piled up on it. 'Where is my bear,' I say lookin for my bear not findin it. 'My bear my Poll Tax Clown.'

Uncle Dustman pickin his nose. 'Who nose.' Uncle Dustman says: 'Could be any where by now. In one of them bags.'

'What is he doin gettin in a bag for.'

Uncle Dustman holdin up his hands what are mucky sayin: 'Im a bit handy. With me hands. Get a bit handy a bit carried away. Start baggin things up.'

Me frownin. Lookin for the bear.

'Any luck.'

'I found him,' I say findin him givin him a hug a bear hug. 'He was under the bags what was on him. On top of him squashin him.'

Uncle Dustman noddin. 'Should still be alright for up ere Tom mate. Snuggle up with them bags.'

Me makin a face.

Then. Jus when I am makin it makin that face. A sound. A ding. Of door bell.

Me lookin at Uncle Dustman. Thinkin: It aint Uncle Dustman dingin door bell comin round ere he is already round ere. It is. Some one what aint round ere. It is. My mum.

'There you go I knew shed be back.' Uncle Dustman says: 'I knew shed see sense. When her fanny gets sore. Go on Tom mate run down there an let her in.'

Me lookin at Uncle Dustman.

'Go on.'

Me goin down stairs doin runnin smilin thinkin about my mum. Then. When I get down it half way down it. Stoppin. Thinkin: It aint her. It aint her.

It aint her. It is. A man a police man. 'Hello mister police man,' I say sayin it to the police man.

Police man noddin. Movin a eye brows pointin em sayin: 'Are your parents in.'

Me shakin head. 'It is jus me,' I say. 'An my uncle my Uncle Dustman.'

Police man noddin. 'Mind if I come in.' Police man not comin in holdin nose it is pointy sayin: 'This uncle. Mind if we have a word.'

Uncle Dustman standin at top of stairs lookin down sayin: 'Give her a hug Tom.'

'It aint my mum,' I say sayin it to Uncle Dustman. 'It is a police man. And. A police lady.' There is a police lady standin next to be side the police man comin up the path.

Uncle Dustman comin down stairs bendin knees got his hands on em gettin handy lookin down the stairs at the police man an police lady.

Police man says: 'Is that your dust cart parked on the road there.'

'Thats right mate yes.' Uncle Dustman sayin it to police man. Then. Lookin at police lady. Smilin. Sayin: 'Alright love.'

Police lady noddin.

Police man sayin: 'Weve received some complaints. From an elderly lady in fact. Two in fact. Its the dust cart. It smells.'

'Thatll be the rubbish. Refuge mainly. House hold waste. Not all rubbish mind you theres some good stuff in there. Amazin what you can pick up. You alright there love.' Uncle Dustman smilin at police lady sayin: 'Mind if I take your coat.'

Police lady not sayin nothin.

'Cheer up love.' Uncle Dustman smilin cheerin her up sayin: 'Might never happen.'

Police lady not smilin. Not cheerin up. He is bein nice cheerin her up but. She wont cheer up. She is a police lady got that police grumps.

Police man pointin at Uncle Dustman makin a point sayin: 'So would you like to move it. Park it down the road there by the flats.'

'Im off in a minute any road.' Uncle Dustman smilin at police lady smilin sayin: 'Fancy comin for a spin. Take your mind off it. Take you out of your self.'

Police lady sayin nothin.

Uncle Dustman frownin sayin: 'Suit your self.'

Police man an police lady turnin blue walkin off.

Uncle Dustman shuttin the door shuttin em out shuttin the spring out shuttin us in it stinks. 'Just my luck. Never did have much luck. With the ladies.'

I am up stairs I am tired. The rubbish stink makin me sleep. Could go down stairs but. There aint no rubbish down stairs. But. Carnt go down stairs I am too tired that rubbish stink makin me sleep. It is dark in my bed room the rubbish bags blockin the window makin it like night time makin me go a sleep. It is the helpin Uncle Dustman what done it. Droppin stuff off makin my arms drop off droppin off.

*

It is mornin I have waked up.

It is mornin but it aint proper mornin. It is a rubbish mornin everythin stink of that rubbish. Even the dream what I made stink of rubbish. It is a dream of my mum cuddlin my mum. Then. When I waked up. I am cuddlin that holdin my nose.

I am got up. Aint layin ere in the stink on the bed what was my bed but aint no more it is rubbish bed.

What time is it. Carnt see out the window the bin bags pilin up on it shuttin it. Still wearin the clobes on the yester day clobes. Didnt even get the jim jams on. Aint gettin dressed if I am dressed. Aint worth it gettin dressed aint.

Me goin down stairs takin my Poll Tax Clown holdin his hand. Carryin him goin down stairs. The light of day light shinin in thru window in front door it is spring it is day time middle of day. I have over slept under the stink of rubbish bin bags of rubbish.

'Uncle Dustman.' Me sayin name of that uncle seein if he is in there. In the stink of rubbish. Where there is rubbish stink of rubbish. There is a uncle what is a dust man. 'Uncle Dustman.'

'In ere Tom mate.'

Me goin in ere. In the front room.

Uncle Dustman is in it. In front room in front of telly. Turnin off the telly doin it quick. It is the video player he is brung it round.

Uncle Dustman gettin back in the chair sittin in it in his under pants what he is got on. It is all what he is got on. Sittin pickin bits out his hair his tummy hair. Pokin his tummy button un button it bum falls off. Laughin. Sayin: 'Been watchin me video.'

'Can I watch it,' I say sayin it nice. 'The video.'

Uncle Dustman shakin his head. 'Adult content.'

'I am a adult. I dont even go a school.'

Uncle Dustman not listenin. 'Thought I better bring it round. If Im gonna be spendin a bit of time ere might as well have it where I can keep me eye balls on it.'

'Are you goin a be ere then. Spendin a bit of time ere.'

Uncle Dustman noddin. 'Well if me video players gonna be ere. Might as well be ere. Keep me eye balls on it.'

'Are you lookin after me then.'

Uncle Dustman scratchin his face. Makin it make thinkin. Shruggin. Sayin: 'Seein as Im ere.'

'Are you makin a break fast.'

'Im watchin me video.'

Me lookin at him a bit funny. 'It aint even on.'

'Not watchin it watchin it.' Uncle Dustman says: 'Watchin it keepin me eye balls on it.'

'O.' Me goin in kitchen makin a break fast. But. Not even goin in it. Lookin in it at what is in it. Lookin at Uncle Dustman sayin: 'Uncle Dustman. What is that in it for. Your plate. With the paintin of a donkey. Doin a pony.'

'Best family silver that is.'

'An the micro wavy overn. An that. That. That mattress.'

Uncle Dustman holdin his nackers sortin em out sayin: 'Didnt I tell you. I sold the house.'

'What house.'

'Me house me room.'

He is sold it. Sellin it. Gettin money. Buyin me a sweets. 'Are you buyin me sweets then,' I say smilin. 'With the money. The sellin the house money.'

'Eh.' Uncle Dustman makin a face. 'O there aint no money Tom mate. Spent it. Bought a pair of under pants.' Uncle Dustman standin up showin me the pants. Turnin round showin em off. They are the bees knees the ants pants the best ones.

'Is that all what it got,' I say. 'The sellin the house money.'

'These are silk these are Tom mate. Lady knocker outers.' Uncle Dustman sittin down dustin down his pants sayin: 'Need all the help I can get. With the ladies. Never did have much luck. With the ladies.'

'I am makin a break fast.'

'Better answer the door first eh Tom mate.'

It is a ding of door bell. Me sayin I am makin a break fast. Uncle Dustman sayin answer it the door. Me goin answer it. Not even thinkin it is my mum.

Uncle Dustman lookin up. At the police man an police lady. Comin in not even sayin nothin comin in. In the front room. In the stink of rubbish.

'Anythin up.'

Police man an police lady not sayin nothin. Then. Police man sayin: 'Would you like to come with us.'

'Anythin up.' Uncle Dustman standin up sayin: 'Mind if I take your coat.' Sayin it to the lady. Showin that pants that lady knocker outers. Knockin her out knock her knockers out.

'Put your trousers on we carnt have you disturbing the peace.' Police man sayin it to Uncle Dustman. 'We have received a further series of complaints. Regarding your vehicle. Regarding. The smell.'

Uncle Dustman gettin a con fuse.

Police man sayin: 'You can stink your own house out as much as you like. But on a public road—'

'Well how longs it gonna take.' Uncle Dustman pointin at me sayin: 'Ive got responsibilities. Im mindin Tom.'

'I think hes old enough to mind him self.'

Me pipin up sayin: 'Am I a adult then.'

'In my book yes.' Police man says: 'In this instance. Yes.'

'Can I watch it then that adult content.'

'What adult content.'

'The video,' I say pointin at video player got video cassette tape in it.

Police man lookin at police lady.

Police lady lookin at police man smilin sayin: 'Maybe we should all watch it.'

Police man standin at the video player bendin knees turnin it on. Pressin try angle button. Turnin it on.

It comin on the telly screen that adult content. It is a field an a writing sayin: Donkey Derby. Bed Ford Shire 1988. Special Collectors Edition. The writin shinin gold like special gold. Then. It is gone that writin is. It is. Donkeys havin a race. Wearin a hat. Walkin. Doin a pony.

Police lady laughin.

Police man turnin it off sayin: 'Each to his or her own. Right then Mister Boler.' Sayin it to Uncle Dustman sayin: 'I am arresting you under section nine nine nine of the Vehicle Odour Act. Put your trousers on thats it. Say good bye to Tom. Good bye Tom.'

Me not sayin nothin. Sayin good bye.

Uncle Dustman sayin bye. Sayin it under a rest.

It is borin it is. Havin a uncle what is under a rest. It is mornin then a after a noon then a evenin then it is a night time an all what I done is. Had a break fast a Anthony Tiger. Eatin it out my Bole bowl my bestest one. Puttin it in my tum. Then. Got ready for goin a school. Thinkin: If I go a school. My mum will come back. But. Then. When I went a school. I didnt even go in it. I got scared. I got scared of school goin in it gettin told off why aint you been school.

What I did is. Didnt do nothin. Sat in arm chair sniffin the stink of what it all stink of. Watchin video cassette tape on video player. It is adult content donkey derby a donkey doin a derby doin a pony. Me watchin it makin it go fast it is the fastest pony what ever that donkey did done.

It is all what I been doin mornin an after a noon an a evenin. Waitin for Uncle Dustman comin back police man an police lady lettin him off hook. Me waitin watchin out the window. Uncle Dustman not comin back not let off hook still on it hangin on it. Hangin on.

Police man comin not that one a other one takin that dust cart drivin it off comfy skatin it same as at school.

Me goin out it is dark goin out in dark. Goin to find my Uncle Dustman. Goin down the road an down nother one an a other one. Findin a police station it is shut.

On it on the door it says: Closed. Then. Next to be side it on the wall is a poster a plastic glass coverin on it. It has got a picture of a police man an he has got a hat on blue pine apple shape like a pine apple what is blue an it says: Remember. We throw away the key.

Then. Next to be side it is a other one sayin: NSPCC. They may be annoying. But they still need to be looked after. The National Society for the Prevention of Cruelty to Children.

Me makin a face a good one bitin lip. Readin it. Then. Readin it again. It is got a picture of a kid a cute one doin cryin. Me lookin at it doin cryin.

Me still standin ere. The cryin still comin out. Comin out like a end of a world but. Me still standin ere.

Primula Spatula

I am in that place that look after place. It is shut but. There is a way in round the back a cat flap. Me goin in it crawlin in it big one aint it. It is big for kids it aint even a cat flap it is a kid flap for kids. Me goin in it in a room what I am in. Goin in it goin a sleep.

Then. When I waked up. Light comin on wakin me up.

Funny this room is. Got walls what are made of wire an a bed what is made of straw. Not a drinkin straw a scare crow hair straw. There is a lot of that sort of rooms each one got a kid in it doin sleepin.

Some one comin. A man an a lady comin in doin a look after. Lady talkin posh sayin: 'Now this one is simply adorable.'

Man noddin his clip board beard noddin his head.

'Simply adorable. Just look at those floppy flappy ears.' Posh lady sayin: 'I could flap them all day. Were it not for wear and tear.'

Me in straw bed bed room lookin out metal caught up wall thinkin: That man. He is the works ere man got clip board. They got too many kids carnt do that much look after. That lady. She is the lady what is customer posh one. Walkin past kids lookin at em sayin: Adorable simply adorable. Then. Stoppin. Lookin. At me.

Clip board man scratchin clip board beard sayin: 'Take your time. And remember. Which ever you choose. Its for life.'

Posh customer lady not sayin nothin. Lookin at that Tom.

Clip board man lookin at posh customer lady catchin her up sayin: 'Whats up.'

Posh customer lady sayin: 'What in the name—'

'Tom,' I say sayin it to the lady.

Clip board man sayin nothin. Lookin at clip board. 'Theres obviously been some sort of cock up.'

Posh customer lady shakin head. 'Hes adorable.' Sayin it to the man. Lookin at me smilin doin it big. 'Simply adorable. Not quite what I had in mind. I admit. But adorable none the less.'

One of them kids doin a joke sayin: 'Woof.'

Posh customer lady walkin me out of look after place openin door. Clip board man standin in it in look after place got mouth open carnt even shut it lettin in the spring. Posh customer lady shuttin it got kid flap in it shuttin it kid flap flappin with the shuttin. Posh customer lady breathin in the spring sayin: 'What an absolutely glorious day.' Holdin my hand walkin me out the fence gate door out in the spring.

Me lookin up at posh customer lady. Thinkin: What a nice posh customer lady.

'I just can not fathom.' Posh customer lady stoppin. Then.

Smilin. Sayin: 'O well you know what they say.' Posh customer lady sayin what they say sayin: 'In for a hound in for a pound.'

'What hound,' I say. 'What pound.'

'How in the name of all things idiotic. Did a boy a real boy. End up in the RSPCA.'

'It is a look after place. A society of children.'

Posh customer lady gettin down bendin knees like police man but police man aint even nice dont even do a look after dont even know what it is. She is nice she is. A lady. With brown hair an curls in it an brown eyes under it. Lookin at me lookin right in a eyes sayin: 'My dear pup. Do you not know what RSPCA stands for.' Posh customer lady standin up findin a sign. It says: RSPCA. A pet is for life. Not just for a laugh. The Royal Society for the Prevention of Cruelty to Animals.

Me makin a face. Lookin at the lady.

'How in the name. Did you end up. In the dog house.'

'I got in it,' I say. 'There is a open up in fence what I open. Then. They got that flap that kid flap.'

'Dog flap.'

'Dog flap. I went in it,' I say sayin it to the lady. 'Then. I went in the straw bed bed room bit an went a sleep.'

'And when did all this happen.'

'I run out a Anthony Tiger a break fast. Got hungry in my tum.'

'Stop there.' Lady makin me stop sayin it sayin: 'Stop right there. We shall go for a bite. To eat. And then. I want you to tell me all about it. The name is Prim by the way.'

'I am Tom Boler I am nine.'

'How fright fully formal.' Prim laughin sayin: 'My name is Primula Spatula. And I am thirty seven. Years. Old. Much to my chagrin. And I am famished.' Prim gettin my hand holdin it sayin: 'I know this little place.'

Me an Prim walkin me down the road holdin hand smilin singin doin it in my head goin in that place that little place. Ethnic minority man standin in try angle shape suit sayin: 'Table for two.'

'One and a half.' Prim sayin it laughin.

Try angle man laughin sayin: 'One and a half yes yes. By the window here we are.' Try angle man movin chair out me sittin on it try angle man movin it in me movin on it. Try angle man gettin a book two of em put em on table.

Me lookin at book. On it it says: Menu. It is borin aint even got colourin in.

Prim lookin at it open it sayin: 'Hump.'

'May I get you something to drink.'

Prim lookin at try angle man sayin: 'The house red.'

'One glass of house red.'

'Bottle.' Prim smilin funny.

Try angle man noddin. 'And for the gentle man.'

Me lookin round. Lookin for a man what is gentle.

Prim reachin over table touchin my hand sayin: 'Tom he means you puppy. What would you like to drink.'

'Squash orange.'

Prim makin a face. 'I dont think they have that. How about an orange squash. Do you have orange squash.'

Try angle man noddin.

'And the set menu for two. Though can you.' Prim laughin sayin: 'Can you make it for one and a half. Tom is only small. A growing pup.'

'Certainly madam. Sir.' Try angle man bendin like tyin shoe lace not doin it walkin off.

Prim lookin at me sayin: 'Now Tom. Lets hear it. Your life story.'

Me makin face.

'Go on.'

'I am Tom Boler,' I say shruggin. 'I am London born an white bread.'

'And what do your parents do.'

'My dad is in prison. On a oil rig. Doin sex.'

'And your mother.'

'Doin sex.'

Prim noddin. 'I see. The less said. Hence the lack of Anthony Tiger. Remind me to purchase a box. On our way home.'

'I aint goin home,' I say sittin up in the chair what the try angle man moved. 'It stinks.'

'Charming.'

'Of rubbish. What my uncle put in it. My uncle what is a dust man my Uncle Dustman.'

'O I see. You meant your home.'

Try angle man bringin squash orange in glass an bottle of wine pour it in a glass put it on table.

'I thought you meant my home. Which positively does not stink. And if it does it is of nice things.' Prim says: 'Such as pot pourri. And joss sticks. From the four corners of the earth. And of course men. Talking of which. What is all this about a dust man.'

'He is my uncle. He is in prison. Every one is. My dad is an my uncle is.'

Prim drinkin wine sayin: 'Thats the working classes for you.'

'They aint even workin. They are doin sex. Even my uncle is doin it havin a luck with the ladies.'

'Is he indeed.'

'He has got. Lady knocker outers.'

'Is that the name of a magazine.'

'It is the name of under pants. Silk under pants,' I say. 'What he has got.'

'And do they work.'

'They aint even workin. They. He is in prison.'

'In silk pants.' Prim laughin sayin: 'That man will be absolutely chock a block with sex.'

'Do they do it in prison then.'

'Sex. One assumes so. I certainly would.' Prim goin funny sayin: 'All those hairy wife beaters.'

'Is that what you like then. Hairy wife beaters.'

'Dont get me started.' Prim gettin started sayin: 'Ah now here comes our starter.'

Me an Prim walkin down the road holdin hands smilin singin fallin over Prim fallin in a bush. Me jumpin on Prim havin fun. It is fun it is. Prim is.

We got our tums full up eatin it all up in that place that little place. Prim drinkin wine gettin tipsy topsy turvy. Me drinkin squash orange gettin tipsy topsy turvy doin it pretend. Prim payin the try angle man pointin gun what shoots money numbers in a laser. Walkin out that place that little place. Then. Fallin. In bush.

Prim gettin out the bush pullin me out it.

Me fallin back in laughin sayin: 'Help I am in it a bush.'

'On the subject of bushes.' Prim laughin sayin: 'You must trim mine for me. When we get home. Assuming we ever make it.'

Me not listenin. Fallin. In bush.

'Youre about the right height.' Prim fallin over sayin: 'I wont even need to stand on a chair.'

Me not listenin. Lookin in shop window.

Prim gettin up catchin me up sayin: 'What. What have you found.'

There is Anthony Tiger piled up. It says: Anthony Tiger breakfast cereal. Half price. While stocks last.

'Well thats a turn up. For the books. Shall we get some.' Prim openin door fallin in it gettin up findin shop man sayin: 'One hundred and fifty boxes. Of Anthony.' Prim fallin over gettin up sayin: 'Tiger.'

The shop man has got a van. We are in it in the van. Me in the back of the van movin about in van back with that one hundred an fifty boxes. Prim in front next to be side van man drivin van. Talkin to the van man sayin: 'Are you married.'

'I am married yes.'

'Happily married.'

'Yes.'

'Bugger.'

Me lookin at one hundred an fifty boxes thinkin: All them Anthony Tiger. It is. Everythin what ever I wanted. My tum thinkin: Yeah I want it in my tum.

Prim openin hand bag sayin: 'Now where did I put my credit gun.' Turnin lookin thru metal square hole bit in van sayin: 'Tom what did I do with my credit gun.'

'You left it in that place that little place.'

'Bugger.' Prim lookin at van man sayin: 'I would lose my own head. If my hair were not so curly. Can I write you a cheque. Tom you wait here. I have to grab my cheque book.' Prim openin front van door gettin out it shuttin it.

Me lookin at Anthony Tiger countin it. One. Two—

61

One—

Front van door openin Prim openin it. Got cheque book flappin smilin sayin: 'Ta daa.'

Prims house is a flat in a posh house in a posh bit of London called Hollow Park. Hollow Park is a lot of houses what are white an got funny shape old fashion shape windows round at the top an square at the bottom. Prims flat is at the bottom. Prim goin down steps openin front door sayin: 'One blushes in shame. All one can say is. In ones defence. It isnt mine.'

It aint a shame. It is posh.

'Mother is dying in November. One week later I move in. Assuming I can get the front door open. Mother is. Or was when she had her health. An avid collector of antiques. Mothers house is full to the brim with the most wonderful junk. Persian cat carpets. Gothic furnishings thru out. And the most delightful collection of poison ivy ever to poison the earth. Now Tom.' Prims eye brows makin a question mark sayin: 'We face a dilemma. How to transfer. One hundred and fifty boxes. Of the cereal with the stripe. From the front garden. To the larder. Whilst under the influence of alcohol. And or orange squash.'

Me thinkin. Doin thinkin face. Then. Sayin: 'We get it. An put it in it.'

Prim goin up steps out in out side out in the spring. She has got a bum a posh one in posh lady trouser. The bum doin smilin. Me goin up the steps smilin at the bum. It smilin sayin: 'I should have asked that man to do it. With those big strong arms.'

Me lookin at the bum.

'There is a lot of it about this time of year. Short sleeves.

Body odour. Hairy chests. Step aside puppy.' Prim pushin the Anthony Tiger down the steps crashin em at the bottom of the steps.

At the bottom of the steps. Me an Prim climbin over the one hundred an fifty boxes. The boxes gettin bent an broke makin Anthony Tiger bits come out gettin on the ground. Me eatin a bit doin it secret goin in kitchen sayin: 'Prim what is a larder.'

Prim in kitchen in larder door makin space in larder sayin: 'In the olden days. Before scientists invented the refrigerator. We had to make do with the larder.' Prim takin things out the larder puttin em back in pilin em up. 'This flat happens to be blessed with both. Refrigerator for perishables. Larder for tinned foods and cereals. Assuming one can make space.'

Me an Prim pickin up the Anthony Tiger carryin it puttin it in larder. Prim has got groan up arms pickin up ten boxes pilin em up. I aint I am little I have got. One box. Pilin up in arms. Me an Prim carryin that Anthony Tiger thru lounge an thru kitchen to the larder. Prim laughin sayin: Dear little pup. Shakin her head doin laughin. Puttin that Anthony Tiger in the larder.

When it is all in the larder Prim shuttin the door standin leanin against the larder door leanin on it. Lookin in lounge sayin: 'We seem to have left a trail.'

'I will follow it,' I say followin it. It is a stripy orange cereal trail got sugar on it an in it.

'Dont eat off the carpet.' Prim says: 'Its uncouth.'

I am a kid but. I am drinkin wine. Me askin for squash orange Prim sayin: I havent got squash erm orange squash. I need to pop to the shop. You can have a drop of my wine.

Just one glass make it last. Me sittin drinkin it makin it last. Prim drinkin it quick makin it not last makin it go to her posh head. Pourin it in the glass drinkin it out the glass. In the posh arm chair got feet up on the posh coffee table. Feet wrigglin smilin. Me in other arm chair got feet up on arm chair carnt even reach the posh coffee table. Carnt even do nothin I am drunk.

'I must say.' Prim sayin it sayin what she must say sayin: 'I rather like the sound of this uncle of yours.'

'Even if he is stinky.'

'Especially if he is stinky. I like a bit of rough.' Prim smilin pourin wine sayin: 'Could even be marriage material.'

'He is in prison,' I say. 'Carnt get married if he is in prison.'

'They wont keep him in there for ever.'

'It will be for ever,' I say doin hic up.

'We dont know that. But we will find out. When they let him out. And if they dont let him out.' Prim stickin her neck out sayin: 'We bust him out.'

Me smilin. Big.

'I would have to get drunk first of course.' Prim drinkin wine gettin drunk sayin: 'We could go to your local police station. To begin with. And ask nicely.'

'Is that where the prison is. At the police station.'

Prim shakin her hair it is brown. 'Do you not know the difference be tween a prison and a police station.'

Me shakin head.

'The difference. Dear pup. Is this. One is full of violent criminals. And the other.' Prim says: 'Is a prison.'

Me noddin head.

'Do you get it.'

Me shakin head. 'When we get him out,' I say. 'Am I got to go home.'

'You are home. Which reminds me.' Prim standin up tippin up doin it drunk. Openin door sayin: 'The sleeping arrangements. Come thru.'

Me gettin up standin up tippin up doin it drunk. Goin in bed room. It is posh got bed shape of love heart. 'It is a nice room,' I say. 'It. That bed. It is a shape like love heart shape.'

'Its a vagina.' Prim says: 'My vagina. Did you not know that Tom that the love heart symbolises the female labia.'

'What bed is my one.'

Prim bitin lip. 'You could sleep in the lounge but there isnt even a couch just the two arm chairs. Now you see why Im ashamed. We could push them together. And throw something over you. Or you could sleep in here with me. At the foot of the bed. With my feet. They may even help you to sleep.'

Me noddin. 'Because of the smell.'

'That wasnt quite what I meant.' Prim wrigglin feet doin it posh. 'I simply meant that you could count my toes. To help you nod off.'

Prim payin taxi driver man with the gun what shoots money numbers in a laser. It is Prims credit gun what she lost it in that place that little place. We went an got it. They are nice in that place that little place.

'Is this the correct police station Tom.'

'That is the one what I went.' Pointin at poster.

Prim lookin at poster. It is got plastic glass coverin on it. It says: NSPCC. They may be annoying. But they still need to be looked after. The National Society for the Prevention of Cruelty to Children. Prim readin it smilin sayin: 'One sees how one as diminutive as you could be taken in. And by some stretch of the imagination. Be taken in as it were. By the RSPCA.'

'Look,' I say pointin at the other one what is next to be side it. It has got a picture of a police man an he has got that hat on blue pine apple shape like a pine apple what is blue an it says: Remember. We throw away the key.

'This does not bode well.' Prim standin hand on hip doin posh tip top tea pot shape sayin: 'But our man is innocent. One assumes. At least. If his vehicle did smell as you say. It smelt in a good cause.'

Me noddin.

'Where would one be. With out working class people. To pick up all the shit.' Prim shruggin sayin: 'Knee deep in it. One would imagine.'

'It aint shit it is general house hold waste.' Me gettin proud doin smilin. 'What he does is. Goes round in that vehicle that dust cart vehicle. Gettin rubbish what is in bags what people put out side their house. Put it in that dust cart. Drive off.'

Prim noddin.

'Or.' Me stoppin smilin. Makin it go up side down. 'What he did. He is in prison.'

Prim noddin. Openin door goin in police station. Then. Comin out sayin: 'Come along puppy heel boy.'

It aint even nice in it. In the police station. There is stink of cigarettes an packet of crisps an fat police man standin be hind counter eatin crisps smoky bacon flavour made of pig. Got blue uniform on wipin hand on it gettin crisp on it on the uniform makin it smell of pig. Sayin: 'You were sayin.' Not sayin it to me an Prim. Sayin it to a lady what is waitin.

Then. Jus when the lady is sayin it sayin what she is sayin. Other police man thin skinny one comin out door out of office out the back sayin: 'Did you see The Bob last night.' Sayin it to the other police man fat one.

Police man fat one not lookin at the lady turnin lookin at police man thin skinny one sayin: 'Whats that that police serial.'

Police cereal.

Prim lookin at me sayin: 'Not that sort of cereal.'

Police man thin skinny one standin be hind police man fat one got thin skinny hand on back of fat chair sayin: 'Yes on the Family Channel after Husbands & House Wifes.'

Police man fat one eatin crisps sayin: 'My wife loves that Husbands & House Wifes.' Police man fat one doin bacon flavour grin sayin: 'When that woman dropped her dog in the swimming pool. My wife wept buckets. I wonder how they filmed it.'

'They wouldve used a stunt dog.'

The lady what is at the counter gettin a red face sayin: 'Erm. Excuse me.'

Police man fat one says: 'You were sayin love.'

'We never used to watch The Bob.' Police man thin skinny one says: 'But then they put it on straight after Husbands & House Wifes—'

The lady what is at the counter gettin cross sayin: 'But what are you goin to do about my husband.'

Police man fat one makin face. Sayin: 'Big chap is he.'

'Big enough to give me this.' The lady liftin up her sun glasses. It is a present what her husband give her. It is. Sun glasses.

Police man fat one lookin at the womans face doin it wrong not lookin at the sun glasses lookin at the womans face. 'Nasty. Drink does he. You want to contact Marriage Menders love. Get signed up. We dont have the um. Resources. Next.'

The woman gettin cross sittin in a chair doin cryin.

Prim standin at the counter sayin: 'We are here to enquire about an arrest made yester day after noon. Surname. Boler. Occupation. Dust man.'

Police man tappin it on computer. Waitin. Pointin. On computer telly screen it says:

Name:	Boler, Harry
Auto-verdict:	guilty, possession of odorous vehicle in built-up area
Auto-sentence:	10 years

'Thats him.' Prim says: 'Thats him. O dear.'

Me sayin: 'Is he in prison.'

Prim noddin. 'Everything happens so quickly these days. Erm. Excuse me madam.' Prim sayin it to the sun glasses lady stopped cryin. Puttin hand on her shoulder whisperin quiet havin a word. When it is finish the havin a word Prim got somethin on a bit of paper the lady wrote it on a bit of paper Prim sayin: 'Come along Tom.'

'What did you say,' I say. 'To the lady.'

'Not for your puppy ears puppy.'

'I aint got puppy ears,' I say touchin ears. 'I got. O. It is puppy ears.'

'Told you.'

Me an Prim sittin in posh wine bar family area. Prim sittin on bar stool at bar got elbows on bar. Me sittin on bar stool got elbows on knee caps got the grumps. Prim drinkin wine sayin: 'We need. To formulate. A plan.'

Me noddin doin it grumpy.

Prim lookin at me sayin: 'Chin up small pup. Where theres a willy. Theres a way. Your uncle does have a willy I take it.'

Me noddin smilin sayin: 'He has got a pants a lady knocker outers. I saw it. It has got a willy in it.'

Prim noddin. 'You saw the bulge. First hand.'

Me noddin. Laughin. 'I have got a little one for kids. Uncle Dustman. He has got a big one same as a dust bin.'

Prim laughin. 'I bet it smells like a dust bin too.'

'It does I smelled it.' Me sayin it a fib. Smilin makin it a fun fib a joke.

'Im not turned on by the smell of rubbish Tom. I want to make that absolutely clear. From the off. Im not turned on by the smell of rubbish. It is the knowledge that my man has returned from a hard days graft. That tugs my tug boat. And nothing brings home that knowledge like an orrible odour.'

Me noddin. Then. Not noddin. Sayin: 'Marco Meccano says girls are smelly.'

'Marco whom.'

'Meccano,' I say. 'He is a His Panic.'

'Well one would. Erm bar man. Another bottle of champagne. And one for the road. We have uncles to rescue.' Prim says: 'The battle for the bulge.'

When we get to the prison. Prim fallin over hittin head on prison. 'Whoops.' Standin up holdin on to side of out side of prison standin up sayin: 'Cover me soldier.'

Me an Prim goin in. Openin the big prison door goin in prison. Prison uniform man standin be hind prison table standin up sayin: 'After noon.'

Prim goin up to the table. Fallin over. Standin up. Holdin on to table sayin: 'We are here to um.' Prim not knowin what to say.

'Are you on a visit.'

'Yes.' Prim flutterin her eye lids sayin: 'We are here to visit one of your in mates. Surname Boler forename Harry.'

Prison uniform man lookin at sheet of paper movin finger down it sayin: 'Ah yes. With the designer under pants.'

Me sayin: 'Can we go an see him.'

Prison uniform man shakin head. 'Not until official visiting time Im afraid.'

Prim gettin in a huff. 'And when is official visiting time.'

Prison uniform man lookin at watch pushin up uniform sleeve makin a groan up grump face lookin at watch sayin: 'Visiting time begins one minute from. Now. Exactly.'

Prim noddin.

Me an Prim waitin.

Prison uniform man lookin at watch.

Me an Prim waitin.

Prison uniform man lookin at watch.

Me an Prim waitin.

Prison uniform man lookin at watch.

Me an Prim waitin.

Prison uniform man lookin at watch. Noddin. Smilin sayin: 'Thru there on the left. First door on the left.'

Me an Prim goin thru first door on the left me gettin left be hind I am little. Prim waitin holdin door. Other prison uniform man lookin in our pockets lookin in Prims hand bag takin things out it puttin em in it. Me an Prim walkin thru door on the left. Walkin past men in prison hairy ones an big. Prim sayin: 'What about him.'

Me shakin head.

'Hes big. He smells. And he has ginormous hands.'

Me shakin head. 'He aint my Uncle Dustman.'

Prim shruggin. 'How about. How about him there with the scar. From ear to here.'

Me shakin head.

'O come on Tom lets just grab a handful and go.'

'It aint a sweet shop,' I say. 'It is a prison.'

'Hmm. How about this one. Hello. What are you in for.'

Prison man in prison lookin at Prim. He is sittin at table other side of table. Other side of table is a woman a wife. Man sayin: 'Whats it to you.'

'Feisty.' Prim clappin hands sayin: 'Super sonic.'

Me lookin at all the prison men in prison. Shakin head. 'He aint even in it.'

'I think they have to unshackle him. We didnt book in advance. Ah here he is.'

'That aint him.'

Prim sittin on chair at other side of table lookin at man smilin sayin: 'Are you Harry.'

Man laughin got black teeth sayin: 'I can be.'

'Well that is handy.' Prim says: 'Harry. When do you get out.'

A woman a wife comin standin by table lookin at black teeth man lookin at sittin down Prim sayin: 'Whos she when shes at home.'

Black teeth man grinnin.

Prim fallin off chair. Prison uniform man two of em pickin her up Prim sayin: 'Man handled.'

Prison uniform man two of em takin her out of prison visit room one of em holdin on her sayin: 'Had a few drinks have we.'

Me sayin: 'I want my Uncle Dustman.'

Prim sayin: 'Yes can we have a dust man.'

Prison uniform man laughin shakin head.

'Then how about a gangster. A rougher upper.'

Me an Prim goin out in street walkin out of it Prim gettin a push helpin her out.

'Desperate times.' Prim says: 'Call for desperate measures. Excuse me while I make a call. Now where did I put my pocket video fone.' Prim openin hand bag sittin on kerb puttin stuff on kerb.

Me sittin on kerb lookin at the stuff. It is. Lip stick. Eye pen. Hair spray. Breath fresh tablets. Sweets. Me lookin at the sweets. They are a round flat ones in square shape sweets wrapper called: Ultra. Me pickin up the sweets sayin: 'Can I eat it.'

Prim shakin head. 'Ah.' Prim takin out pocket video fone pickin up bit of paper got a number on it an a name.

Prim is a groan up doin a groan up thing. It is what I am goin to do when I am groan up. It is. Goin on a hot date. A hot date is what you go on a hot date. It is. Super sonic. Havin a long soak put your feet up. Doin your make up. Choosin a out fit. Havin a hair cut down below. Me doin the hair cut down below sayin: 'What are you goin to do on it. On that goin on a hot date.'

Prim tappin her nose sayin: 'Lets just say. It will involve. Fine wine. Wandering hands. And a candle lit dinner for two. Not. I might add.' Prim laughin sayin: 'Two and a half.'

'Can I go on a hot date.'

Prim pointin eye points. 'You didnt listen to a word I just said did you.'

Me shakin head.

'Tom you know I would take you if I could but I simply can not. The table is booked for two. I did ask if they had a table for two and a half but.' Prim sighin doin it posh. 'I tell you what I will do.' Prim brushin off cut hair caught. Brushin it off. Puttin on a dressin gown. Standin. At table dresser dressin table. Got a ball not a foot ball one a posh one it is class it is glass. Movin hands on it sayin: 'I will look. In to. My crystal ball.'

'What are you lookin in to it for,' I say lookin in to it.

Prim lookin in to crystal ball sayin: 'It tells the future. Thats funny.' Prim scratchin curly brown hair sayin: 'You dont seem to have one.'

'Aint you got a turn it on.'

Prim turnin it on sayin: 'Ah. Right now what have we got.'

'Am I goin on a hot date.'

Prim noddin. Smilin. Sayin: 'Yes Tom yes. With a girl.'

'Is she pretty.'

Prim sayin nothin. Makin a face. 'She has a nice personality.'

'What is she doin.' Me havin a look. O.

'Its a natural bodily function Tom.' Prim havin a look tellin me what she is doin. 'Shes finished now shes wiping. Very thorough. And thats a good thing Tom isnt it.'

Me noddin.

'You know what they say.' Prim sayin what they say sayin: 'Clean on the toilet dirty in bed. Or is it the other way round. Hang on this isnt even the right girl. Heres one for you.'

Me gettin a hope up.

'Enjoys colouring books hole games and mucking about. And something called lick bits. What ever that is. Would like to meet boy three years her senior for LTR.'

'Whats that,' I say. 'That LTR.'

'Long term relationship Tom long term relationship.' Prim sniffin her nose doin it posh sayin: 'We all want one of those. Though two would be better. In parallel not in serial.'

'I like cereal.'

'Im glad to hear it Tom theres one hundred and fifty boxes in the larder.'

It is borin on a hot date. Sittin in arm chair. Eatin Anthony Tiger. Drinkin squash orange in groan up wine glass. On a hot date. On a own.

I am watchin telly for groan ups. It is the news it is borin. Then. When it goes off. A other one comin on. It is. Real Red Hot Dates.

'Hello and welcome to Real Red Hot Dates.' It is on the telly in a telly studio on telly. A smilin lady called Nan Nosy smilin sayin: 'Im Nan Nosy. Over the coming weeks. We will be joining six red hot couples as they go on a series of six red hot dates. This week. I would like you to meet. Prunella. Our first lucky lady.' Nan Nosy movin her hand showin a lady.

That lady. She is like Prim. She aint Prim but she is like Prim. Prunella is a fat posh lady Prim is a thin one got thin posh bum. Prunella got fat posh bum tum smilin sayin: 'Hello.'

Nan Nosy smilin. 'Hello Prunella and welcome to the show.'

'Hello.'

'Are you nervous Prunella.'

Prunella smilin shakin her head movin her hair sayin: 'No. Well. Maybe a bit.'

'And now. It is time to meet our first lucky man your red hot date.' Nan Nosy movin her hand showin a man sayin: 'This. Is Peter Shitton.'

The man noddin. Smilin. Not sayin nothin.

'Peter Shitton is an estate agent from Dun Roamin. Hello Peter and welcome to the show.'

Peter Shitton noddin.

'Are you nervous Peter.'

Peter Shitton shruggin. Smart suit movin with the shruggin. Sayin: 'Um.'

I am eat a Anthony Tiger. Eatin it all up. Eatin a whole box. Tippin it in bowl eatin it tippin it in bowl eatin it gettin a tum ache. Eatin it all up. Watchin that Real Red Hot Dates.

Nan Nosy in posh eat place movin her hand showin a posh table sayin: 'Lets leave them to it.'

Prunella an Peter Shitton sittin at posh table. Openin napkin puttin it on lap on trouser. Prunella puttin it on lap on dress it is a out fit like what Prim got. Prunella sayin: 'Well.'

Peter Shitton sayin: 'Well.'

Prunella noddin. Smilin. Sayin: 'Here we are.'

'Indeed.'

Prunella movin hair. Doin it pretty. 'Erm. So what made you become an estate agent.'

Peter Shitton thinkin. Makin thinkin shape on table. 'Hmm.'

'Did you always want to be an estate agent.'

'I think I. I think I always—'

'Since you were very young.'

Peter Shitton noddin.

Nan Nosy sayin: 'The waiter is about to bring the main course.'

Prunella an Peter waitin eatin main course. That is what Prim is doin that is. Eatin main course. In a posh eat place. On a red hot date.

Me eatin Anthony Tiger. On it it says: Ingredients. Sugar. Reconstituted cereal extract. It says: Special offer. Collect

150 tokens and claim your FREE box of Anthony Tiger. The cereal with the stripe.

Me gettin Anthony Tiger one hundred an fifty boxes gettin em out of larder. Cuttin out token. Cuttin box an cuttin in box bag in box. Anthony Tiger fallin out. Then. When it is all cut out fallin out. Prunella an Peter Shitton goin out. Walkin at a river. Holdin hands. Peter Shitton sayin: 'Well.'

Prunella smilin sayin: 'Well.'

'Shall we um. Would you like to.' Peter Shitton sayin: 'Get married.'

Prunella noddin. Smilin. Havin a kiss.

Door openin Prim comin in. Turnin light on wavin at it sayin hello. Fallin over.

Man comin in. He is big got arms got drawin on it in cartoon. Comin in. Fallin over. Landin on Prim.

'Lets do it here. On the carpet.' Prim says: 'Covered in break fast cereal.'

Big cartoon arm man lookin at me sayin: 'Whos that.'

Prim lookin at me wavin hand sayin: 'Tom. Hello Tom.'

I am in arm chair havin a sleep. Turned telly off an light off an havin a sleep. Then. I am got waked up.

Big cartoon arm man standin up sayin: 'Can we get to bed. Been on the site all day. Know what I mean.'

Prim standin up pullin man up pullin belt open it hold it out pullin it out sayin: 'Night Tom.'

It is cold on a arm chair on a own. Me gettin off arm chair goin in bed room gettin in love heart shape bed. Gettin in the foot of the bed. Countin Prims feet goin asleep.

One. Two—

One—

Prim is a posh lady got posh pretty lady feet. That man. That cartoon arm man. He is big got big feet.

One—

Me tryin doin countin but. Feet keep movin. That man. Got them feet mixed up the pretty lady feet an man ones what a man got.

It is mornin it is time for break fast. Prim pourin milk in Anthony Tiger tippin it in plate. Prim in kitchen me sat up kitchen table watchin kitchen telly it is small. On it it has got. Advert. There is kids eatin break fast cereal it is nice it is Crunchy New Internet Shapes. Kids lookin at mum gettin smile. Their mum. She aint even havin sex. She is with kids gettin smile.

Prim sayin: 'Thursday is a school day isnt it.'

Me noddin.

'Is there something wrong puppy.' Prim sayin: 'You dont seem to be eating your Anthony Tiger.'

Me lookin at Anthony Tiger. Movin spoon. Not even eatin.

Prim puttin water melon on plate tuckin in doin it groan up. Then. Lookin at me sayin: 'Not hungry small pup.'

Me shakin head. Not even hungry.

'But theyre your favourite.'

Me shakin head.

'Theyre not your favourite.' Prim makin face sayin: 'Then what are your favourite.'

Me lookin at Anthony Tiger. Sniffin. Then. Sayin: 'Internet one.' Pointin at telly.

Prim lookin in other room. At Anthony Tiger one hundred an fifty boxes cut up. Sayin: 'Bugger.'

*

That man. That big cartoon arm one. He is in bed. Havin a lay in a day off. Prim sayin: 'Go and play puppy. I have a man to attend to. After shagging him in to an early grave. The least I can do. Is resuscitate him.'

That man. He is a man a work man.

That is what I want to be when I grow up. A man a work man.

I am goin to work. Walkin down street what is broke. Findin a house what is broke. Findin a man a work man sayin: 'Are you a work man.'

'Hello.' Work man pattin me on head sayin: 'Shouldnt you be at school.'

'It is a day off.'

Work man noddin. He has got. Orange short shorts. Orange tee shirt. Orange mos tosh. He is a man a work man.

'Are you a work man.'

'Im a builder.' Builder sayin: 'A day off you lucky thing. I wish I could take a day off.'

'That other one is. That one what Prim is shagged.'

'Prim.'

'She is a lady a posh lady,' I say. 'She looks after me she does.'

'Does she indeed.'

Me noddin. Sayin: 'Im a builder I am.'

'Are you indeed.'

Me noddin.

Builder lookin at watch sayin: 'Well then youd better get to work then hadnt you. You see this house. We have to build three more of these by lunch time. Think youre up to it.'

Me noddin.

'Whats your name.'

'Tom,' I say sayin it my name.

'Come along Tom.' Builder laughin sayin: 'Come and meet the boys.'

The builder he is called Lesley. It is a girl name same as a girl. Lesley takin me to meet the boys. Takin me in house what is broke. Sayin: 'This is Marty. Say hello Marty.'

Marty sayin: 'Hello Marty.'

'And this is Patsy. Say hello Patsy.'

Patsy sayin: 'Hello Patsy.'

Patsy is a builder a man a black man got flat black tum an a ants in a pants. Me lookin at pants sayin: 'They are like my uncles.'

'What these things.'

Me noddin. 'He is got them ones the same one.'

Patsy gettin up standin up. He is sit on tool box eatin sand witch. Patsy standin up showin me the pants black pants got ants in. Patsy standin up standin on tool box doin dancin. Shakin pants. They are pants like under pants.

'What you doin.'

'Dancing.' Patsy shakin pants sayin: 'Swish.'

'What are you dancin for,' I say. 'Aint you a builder doin buildin.'

Patsy not sayin nothin. Doin dancin.

Marty holdin up cup of tea cup sayin: 'Tea break.' Holdin up tea cup movin it doin tea dancin tea.

'All builders like to dance.' Patsy sayin it shakin pants.

'They dont.'

'Then what do they like. We like.'

Me shruggin. 'Foot ball.'

Patsy laughin.

'Havin a fight,' I say.

Patsy laughin. Slappin flat black tum.

Marty sayin: 'Patsy and I fight dont we Patsy.'

Patsy laughin. Not sayin.

Lesley turnin orange mos tosh sayin: 'All couples fight Patsy.'

Patsy laughin.

'Are you boy friend and girl friend then.' Me sayin it to Patsy. Sayin it to Marty.

'Boy friend and girl friend my ass.' Patsy slappin black pants ass sayin: 'Do I look like a girl to you.'

Me noddin.

Thinkin.

Thinkin of somethin what some one said at school. Sayin: If you are a boy. An you kiss a boy. Or. Sit next to a boy. At school. You are a gay. 'Are you a gay.' Me sayin it to Patsy.

Patsy laughin. Slappin tum.

Me bitin lip.

Lesley puttin arm round me sayin: 'All builders are gay Tom.'

Me makin face.

'Didnt you know.'

Me shakin head. Didnt even know.

'Thats because we keep it a secret.' Lesley says: 'When ever a pretty girl walks past—'

Patsy lookin out of house lookin at girl. Puttin fingers in mouth. Doin whistle.

'We whistle.' Lesley says: 'Then. When theres no one about. We dance. And prance about. In gay abandon.'

Patsy laughin fallin over doin it like Prim but. A man a gay.

'What about. What about that one what Prim is shagged.

He is a man a work man. He is big. He is. Hairy.' Me holdin out arms doin shape of hairy.

Lesley pullin face.

'He is got drawins on a arms,' I say showin arm. 'In cartoon.'

Lesley noddin. 'Perhaps he isnt a real builder.' Lesley turnin orange mos tosh sayin: 'Some lesser breed of work man. A road sweeper perhaps. Or a litter picker.'

'A litter what er.'

'A litter picker. A litter picker upper. If he isnt gay.' Lesley says: 'Its highly unlikely hes a builder.'

'But,' I say. 'If. If you are a gay. That is like. A girl.'

'And.'

'Girls carnt do build,' I say. 'It is men.'

Patsy laughin doin antsy pantsy pansy pants dance. 'Girls can build. We can build carnt we Marty.'

Marty noddin. Wrigglin hip. Gettin a brick. Givin it to Patsy. Patsy doin dancin movin brick movin it makin it do dance. Puttin it on wall. Makin it part of wall.

'Can I do a build.'

Marty puttin hand on hip doin tea pot drinkin tea.

Patsy sayin: 'If you think youre man enough.'

'I am man enough,' I say sayin it a fib. 'I am a man a adult.'

Patsy doin nod sayin: 'First. You choose a brick. Any brick. And position it on the wall like so.' Patsy gettin brick. Puttin it on wall. Like so. Like. A girl a gay.

Me lookin at brick pile of brick.

'Hurry up.' Patsy sayin: 'We havent got all day.'

Me pickin up a brick. Droppin it is heavy.

'Ooo I thought you said you were a man.'

Marty laughin. 'Hes more of a man than you are dear.'

'You can talk.' Patsy puttin hand on my shoulder. 'Try again Tom. Careful this time. Im wearing open toe shoes.'

Me lookin at shoes. What Patsy got. They are open toe got toe pokin out got on it nail polish. Me pickin up brick doin it careful. Got it two hands. Liftin it up. Put it on wall.

Patsy laughin sayin: 'The other way. Turn it the other way.'

Me lookin at brick. It pokin out pokin out of wall. Me turnin it a other way.

'Now.' Patsy clappin hands. 'Apply the semen.'

Marty says: 'He means the cement. Hes showin off arent you Pats.'

Patsy laughin. Showin off.

'Here let me demon straight.' Marty puttin down tea. Standin up. Holdin a hand puttin it on thing what is metal made of wood. 'You take your trowel.' It is a trowel a metal wood one. Me takin it Marty makin me take it. 'You take your trowel. Your cement. A generous amount dont be shy.' Marty puttin it in semen cement gettin it on trowel. 'And. Apply.'

Patsy sayin: 'Dont forget to smooth.'

Me lookin at Marty.

Marty noddin. 'Go on.'

Patsy sayin: 'Smooth dear smooth.'

Me gettin trowel. Puttin it on brick on semen cement. Movin it makin it flat like hat put it on head.

Marty noddin. 'Good.'

Me smilin. Sayin: 'Im a builder aint I.'

'Almost.' Patsy says: 'But not. Quite. In order to become a fully qualified builder. We need. To see. You dance.'

'No,' I say. 'I aint doin dancin. It is for girls dancin is.'

'How can it be for girls.' Patsy says: 'And who dances with these girls.'

'Boys.'

Patsy clappin hands sayin: 'Right. So. There for. Strip down to your under pants.'

Me strippin down to under pants. Takin off a trouser. Puttin it on wall on brick wall gettin on it a semen cement. Standin. In pants.

'Follow my lead.' Patsy sayin: 'You put your left leg in.' Patsy puttin left leg in sayin: 'Come on youre not following.'

Me puttin left leg in.

'Thats right. Hand on hip.'

Me puttin hand on hip.

'Blow me a kiss.'

Me blowin Patsy a kiss.

'And your right leg goes out like so.' Patsy puttin right leg out like so. 'And you do the splits.' Patsy doin the splits showin bum showin the hole sayin: 'And every one sees your bum.'

Marty says: 'Patsy you are such a slut.'

Patsy standin up. Doin eye brow shape shape of cross.

'You are Patsy youre a slut. Always putting it about.'

'Im supposed to be putting it about. Im dancing.' Patsy doin dancin sayin: 'In out in out put it all about.'

'I dont mean that. Youve changed Patsy. Ever since you had your cheeks emphasised. I hardly recognise you.'

'O and you can talk.' Patsy pointin the finger sayin: 'Look at you with your chest furniture. And your boob bum tit lift.'

'At least Im not a slut.'

Patsy an Marty havin a fight. Patsy slappin face of Marty. Marty grabbin pants of Patsy. Patsy pokin out tongue. Marty spittin at Patsy. Patsy pullin hair of Marty. Then. Lesley. Twistin twirlin tosh it is orange. Steppin in be tween Marty an Patsy. Breakin it up sayin: 'Break it up break it up.'

Patsy an Marty breakin it up.

'Youre a disgrace to your sexuality.' Lesley tellin em off sayin: 'Now I want you two to bury the hatchet and make up.'

Patsy shakin head.

Marty lookin at Patsy. Shakin head.

'Youve survived bigger tiffs than this.' Lesley holdin out little finger wrigglin it sayin: 'Little pinkies.'

Marty holdin out little finger sayin: 'Little pinkies.'

Patsy holdin out little finger. 'Ive got a little brownie.'

Marty laughin.

Lesley sayin: 'Thats better.'

Patsy an Marty holdin out fingers puttin it round finger.

Lesley sayin: 'Thats it repeat after me. Make up make up. Never never break up.'

Patsy an Marty sayin it sayin: 'Make up make up. Never never break up.'

'Now kiss.' Lesley says: 'And make up.'

Patsy sayin: 'Dont smudge my make up.'

Marty an Patsy doin kiss.

Me shakin head.

Lesley lookin at me laughin at me at my head shake shape. 'If you think builders are gay Tom. You should meet our roofer.' Lesley pointin up at roof at roofer. 'Shirley. Formerly known as Charlie.'

Me makin face. Dont like it.

Me goin up up there up on roof. To get on it. You have to do runnin on scaffolding climbin up ladder up scaffolding jumpin over barrels Shirley Charlie throwin em rollin em down scaffolding. Me jumpin over em gettin a points. It is a game get a points dont get killed. Me jumpin up gettin hammer hit it on barrels makin it get killed. Me climbin ladder gettin at top.

At the top. There is a roofer a man got dress on. Standin on roof got dress on got on it flowers got arms hairy like a monkey. He is Shirley Charlie he is hairy a monkey.

'Are you a monkey,' I say sayin it to Shirley Charlie.

Shirley Charlie sayin: 'Grrr.'

Me steppin back. Holdin up hands. 'I am Tom I am little.'

Shirley Charlie noddin. Sayin: 'Gr.'

Me sayin: 'Are you a man.'

Shirley Charlie shakin head. Sayin: 'Grrr.'

'Can I come an see you.'

Shirley Charlie lookin at me doin it careful. Standin up. Holdin out arms hittin chest. Then. Sittin down. Noddin. Sayin: 'Gr.'

Me walkin doin it slow sittin down next to be side him. 'Are you a man.'

'Grrr.'

'A woman a lady.'

'Gr.'

Me noddin. He is a woman a lady.

'Are you up on a roof.'

'Gr.'

Me lookin down. Lookin at road. It is down there down in a road. I aint I am up ere up on a roof up in a air. It is fresh air it is spring. Air gettin in hair makin it move like spring a spring doin sprung. 'It is high up,' I say. 'Aint it.'

'Gr.'

'Are you scared. Of that high up.'

'Grrr.'

'Have you ever fallen down.'

'Grrr.'

Me noddin. He aint fallen down he is good at it a roofer. I aint I aint even good at it. 'Can I be a roofer. I am good at it at learnin. Can you learn me be a roofer.'

Shirley Charlie lookin at me careful. Holdin out hand it is hairy. Holdin it on my head. I am little too little aint even allowed.

'What about. When I am groan up.'

Shirley Charlie doin thinkin. Sittin. Lookin. At sky it is blue high up. Then. Lookin. At me. Shruggin. Raisin a eye brow raisin roof. Sayin: 'Gr.'

Me runnin down the steps knockin on door of flat.

Prim openin door hidin be hind it sayin: 'Yes.'

'It is me,' I say. 'Tom.'

Prim openin door openin it lettin me in. Prim wearin sun glasses.

Me gettin excited sayin: 'Prim guess what I am.'

'A puppy.'

'No,' I say shakin head. 'I am. What I am is. A builder.'

Prim not sayin nothin. Not gettin excited. 'Tom please dont be a builder. I dont like builders.'

'But—'

'Ive had it up to here with builders.'

Me lookin around room. 'Where is that man. That builder.'

Prim not sayin nothin.

Me lookin in other room. In bed room. He aint there. 'Where is he gone,' I say. 'That builder.'

'He gave me this.' Prim pointin at sun glasses. It is a sun glasses a present what he give her. Pointin at door sayin: 'So I showed him the door. And now. I am going to bed. For a good old fashioned cry.'

Poll Tax Clown

Prim comin out of bath room sayin: 'Tom. Time to get up
for school.' Then. Goin back in bath room brushin teeth
spittin it out. Comin out of bath room. 'Tom.' Goin back
in bath room. Sittin on bog loo toilet seat. Doin pee. Singin
a song a bog loo toilet song doin pee. Standin up. Comin
out of bath room pullin up knickers groan up ones sayin:
'Tom are you awake puppy.'

Prim openin bed room door lookin in bed room. 'Tom.'
It is a bed heart shape it is posh. Prim. Liftin heart shape
silk bed sheet. Lookin at that Tom but. There aint even a
Tom.

Prim lookin under bed lookin for that Tom sayin: 'Tom
are you hiding. Is this a game. Are we playing hide and seek.'

Prim goin in lounge lookin be hind arm chair an other arm
chair a other one. Lookin be hind telly. Puttin on slippers
and dressin gown. Openin front door. Goin up steps. Lookin

up an down street it is posh it is Hollow Park. Foldin a arms. Shakin head. Sayin: 'Tom.' Shoutin it gettin cross.

Prim goin back in flat shuttin door. Sittin. On a arm chair. Holdin hand on head havin a think.

Then.

It comin a idea.

Prim standin up. Goin in kitchen. Openin larder door lookin in larder it is empty. Aint even a Anthony Tiger. It is in rubbish bin it is rubbish.

Prim shuttin larder door. Openin a cubberd a high up one for groan ups. Gettin out a cereal box of cereal. It is a new one it is. Crunchy New Internet Shapes. Prim gettin it tippin it in bowl. Pourin in a milk. 'Tom. Crunchy New Internet Shapes.'

Then. Jus when she is sayin it. Larder door openin me comin out lookin at bowl.

Prim lookin at me careful. 'How did. How did—'

Me smilin. Not even sayin.

Prim openin larder door of larder. Lookin in it is empty.

'Tom do you possess magical powers. Are you some form of diminutive magician.'

'Yeah I am. On a school day I am. When I dont want a go a school.'

'Crafty.' Prim puttin spoon in Crunchy New Internet Shapes. Havin a eat. 'Tom puppy these are foul.'

Me sittin up table.

Prim puttin bowl on table. Pickin up box lookin at it doin read. 'And no wonder.' Puttin box on table. Openin fridge gettin out it a lemon.

Me eatin Crunchy New Internet Shapes. Lookin at box. On it it says: Ingredients. Saccharin. E numbers. Edible plastic base. It says: Log on. To the crunchiest internet shaped new cereal.

Prim eatin lemon an drinkin water a glass of water.

Me doin yawn.

'Couldnt you sleep puppy.'

Me shakin head. Doin it sleepy.

'Didnt you count my toes. I told you to count my toes.'

Me noddin. 'I counted it,' I say sayin it clever. 'There is two.'

'Dear you counted my feet. Toes are a subdivision of feet. No wonder you couldnt sleep.' Prim shakin brown hair head. 'Perhaps you had better return to bed. Youre nodding off in to your cereal.'

Me puttin head in Crunchy New Internet Shapes. Goin a sleep.

'We carnt have you snoring in the class room.'

Me liftin head liftin it out of Crunchy New Internet Shapes. Shakin it shakin head.

Prim takin bowl. 'Here let me take that.'

'No,' I say tryin an takin it. 'I am goin a eat it.'

'But youre too tired puppy dog.'

'I aint,' I say tryin an take it.

Prim standin up holdin bowl up sayin: 'If I give you your cereal. Will you go to school.'

Me shakin head. Doin a yawn doin it pretend.

'So youre too tired for school. But you can muster up the energy to eat your cereal.'

Me noddin.

'I see. Now this is what they call selective tiredness.' Prim shakin brown curl hair. 'Tom this really isnt good enough. We none of us like Monday mornings puppy but this is taking the piss. Eat up and lets get you ready. Wheres your school uniform.'

'At my house,' I say eatin up.

'Well we dont want to go any where near that place. It sounds utterly horrid. A father in prison. A mother. Running off every five minutes. With the milk man.' Prim wipin a eye. 'Eat up. We shall pop to the shop. And purchase you a school uniform brand bottom spanking new.'

Me an Prim walkin in door of shop. Me an Prim stoppin in shop. Prim clappin her hands sayin: 'School uniform. Super sonic.'

'No,' I say. 'It is rubbish school uniform is.'

Prim closin her eye brows. 'Tom puppy—'

Carnt hear. Gone out side.

Prim followin sayin: 'Tom dont be such a—'

Me out side shop lookin up at name of shop. It says: Wool Woofs.

'Puppy dog what are you doing.'

'Look,' I say pointin at other shop over a road. 'A groan up shop. For groan ups.'

'Yes and youre a little boy now get back in here before I make you even littler.'

Me lookin at shop. Thinkin about bein groan up. Thinkin: When I am groan up. I—

Prim pullin me in shop makin me go in. It is rubbish shop it is for kids. Prim gettin school uniform holdin it up. 'These trousers. About your size. Give or take a few turn ups. Tom. Tom—' Prim liftin up skirt of fat woman pullin me out I am hidin. 'Tom what is it about school that you so detest.'

Prim takin me to school walkin me up to gate. Me standin at gate doin cryin. Prim walkin me up to class room. Me not goin in class room. Doin cryin. Not goin in. Prim sayin: 'Why puppy. Why dont you want to go in.'

'It is ages. I will get told off.'

'Nonsense wait here.' Prim goin in. Goin up to teacher Miss Kind goin up to desk gettin told off. Havin a word with Miss Kind. Comin out puttin a arms round sayin: 'Ive had a word with Miss Kind. She isnt cross. I told her that there had been a family crisis in the family. But that it is all over and not to worry.'

Me noddin. Lookin in window.

All them other kids. They are in there. It is after a noon.

'In you go.' Prim openin class room door pushin me in doin it nice. 'Be a big brave puppy for Primula.'

Me goin in. Not even doin it brave. Doin it cryin. Wipin it on a eye. Gettin that cry on uniform it is new.

Every one lookin at me. Lookin at that cry.

When I am goin in it. It gettin bigger. It is. A biggest class room what ever I ever been goin in.

Then. Miss Kind sayin: 'Tom youve joined us just in time. For. Story time.'

Every one gettin up jumpin up shoutin: 'Yeah.'

Me gettin up standin up not shoutin it. Lookin at window. Where there aint that Prim.

Every one goin over to carpet. It is in corner it is big. Every one doin sit on it. It is what you sit on doin story. It is nice on it. It has got books on it on shelf got pictures in it. It has got cushion on it every one sit on it on cushion. Miss Kind sittin on it every one sit on it on cushion. Miss Kind sittin on it on chair on carpet. 'Today. We will do things a little differently.'

Every one lookin. Lookin at Miss Kind. Thinkin: It is difrent. Where is that book that story book. She aint got it is difrent.

'Every one close your eyes.'

Every one closin eyes doin it shut.

'This carpet. Is actually a magic carpet. When you close your eyes. It floats out of the window and up in to the sky and soars over magical lands and cities.'

Every one shuttin eyes. Sayin: 'Wow.'

'But the thing about magic carpets.' Miss Kind sayin that thing sayin: 'Is this. If you want the magic to work its magic. You have to wish for it.'

Every one makin wish. One of them a girl doin whisper sayin: 'Please magic carpet please.'

'The thing about. Sally close your eyes. The thing about magic carpets is. The magic only works with your eyes closed. If you open your eyes. The magic stops. And you find your self back in the class room.'

The boy what is next to be side me puttin hand up sayin: 'How we gonna get back.'

Miss Kind sayin it kind sayin: 'The carpet will deliver you safely to the ground. In an instant.'

The boy what is next to be side me. He is called. Andrew Hand. Andrew Hand puttin hand next to be side my ear doin whisper sayin: 'Muck about pass it on.'

'No,' I say sayin it a whisper. 'I will get told off.'

'Pass it on.' Andrew Hand sayin: 'Go on.'

'Andrew Hand if I have to tell you one more time. Andrew sit with me at the front. Where I can keep my eye on you.'

Andrew Hand gettin told off. Standin up. Steppin over knee caps an shoe legs. Walkin. Sittin. With Miss Kind.

Sally puttin hand up sayin: 'Miss Kind. Miss Kind if we have got our eyes closed. We wont see the countries and cities.'

'You have to picture them. In your minds eye. Try it now.' Miss Kind sayin: 'You should feel the ground drop away beneath you. And. As the carpet rises. You see the play ground and the school buildings as small as ants—'

Me shuttin my eyes. Picturin it in my minds eye but—

'—the people the trees—'

—all what I can see is—

'—the cars and buses—'

—my mum—

'—hills valleys—'

—doin sex tellin me off.

Then. When I open my eyes. I carnt see it I carnt see that sex.

What I can see is. Miss Kind got eyes shut doin talkin. Every one got a eyes shut. Not even lookin. Not seein that magic what is a other one. It is a magic floor me doin crawlin on it crawlin on floor. Hidin. Be hind book case. Standin. Openin door. Runnin out door doin runnin runnin out in the spring.

That runnin. It aint even my fault. It is magic makin me do runnin gettin a way. Runnin on that play ground on that path what Prim walked on tellin me off tellin me go a school get told off.

Me runnin be hind shops. Lookin be hind me. There aint no one be hind me. Me runnin be hind shops runnin stoppin gettin a breath back. Lookin be hind me. Be hind shops.

Be hind the shops. There is a plastic wire fence what is broke got hole in. Me goin in hole. It is small for kids your mum carnt fit in it she is fat. Me goin in bush roots under em slidin gettin caught up in bush roots slidin down dirt under bush roots gettin caught up.

Then. Comin out in park.

In the park. There is a lot of big boys smokin cigs. One of em pointin at me sayin: 'Oi ask that kid.'

Me standin up. Brushin that dirt mud off an class room floor dust off brushin it off. It is on school uniform it is new.

Them other lot of big boys. Groin an Thick Ear an Hair Cut. They are at little end of Big School. This lot. They are proper big boys. At big end of it leavin school gettin groan up gettin a job.

'Oi.' One of em shoutin it shoutin: 'Oi.'

Me lookin at big boys thinkin: If I talk to em. They will beat me up. But. If I dont talk to em doin runnin a way. They will run after me me fallin over hittin head on park.

One of big boys comin over. 'You got a light.' Holdin cig puttin it in mouth movin it about.

Me shakin head. Puttin hand on school uniform it is new. Lookin for a light.

Big boy lookin at me. Movin cig movin it in mouth. Lookin at me lookin for a light. Lookin in that school uniform it is new.

It aint in it is it.

'Oi lamer.' Other boy tall one comin over. 'Oi lamer you got a light or aint you.'

Me shakin head.

'Then what you lookin in your pockets for. Either you got a light. Or you aint.'

Me shakin head. 'I aint.'

'You aint. What you mean you aint. Thats out of order aint it Bricks.' Tall boy sayin it to other boy.

Other boy noddin. 'Yeah we should bust him.'

Tall boy punchin me on arm sayin: 'Busted.'

'Ow,' I say holdin it on arm.

'Busted nice one.' Bricks sayin it noddin head.

Me doin big boy talk sayin: 'Oi fuckin ell.'

Tall boy laughin at me at what I said. 'Oi you aint allowed to swear at your age is he Bricks.'

Bricks noddin. 'Yeah we should bust him.'

Tall boy punchin me on arm doin it again sayin: 'Busted.'

'Ow.'

Bricks laughin.

Tall boy laughin.

Bricks movin cig sayin: 'Oi where we gonna get a light then.'

'Get him to get it.'

Bricks gettin money out of out of shape trouser pocket givin me it. 'Oi theres some dollar.'

Me lookin at money got it in hand.

'Go on then.' Tall boy slappin me on back makin me fall over. 'Oi matches up you go.' Slappin me on back pushin me up dirt bush root bit.

'Oi what if he dont come back.'

Tall boy grabbin my unkle leg. 'Oi give us your blazer.'

'I carnt,' I say. 'It is new.'

'Take it off. Or I bust you.'

Me takin it off.

Tall boy hittin me on arm.

Bricks laughin. 'But he give you it.'

'Shut it lamer.' Tall boy hittin Bricks on arm. 'Now youre both busted.' Tall boy pushin me up dirt bit sayin: 'Get up there an get them matches. If you aint back in ten. Im wearin your blazer.'

In the sweet shop. There is a lady a cross one what gets cross. When it is goin home time. Kids comin out of school comin in shop. The lady gettin cross at kids it is too many kids. The kids. Gettin told off cross lady tellin em off.

'Have you got a matches a light.' Me sayin it to cross lady.

Cross lady lookin at me. Gettin cross. 'What you want matches for.'

'It is for big boys,' I say sayin it. 'They told me to get it. They gave me money for it.' Me holdin out that money.

Cross lady lookin at money. Lookin at me at my age. Cross lady sayin: 'I dont usually sell matches to school children. Matches are dangerous.'

'But that boys.' Me pointin at door. 'It is dangerous. They will beat me up.'

'Well dont play with them then.'

'They have got my blazer. He is goin a wear it make it get broke.'

'Isnt that blackmail.'

'No he is white a white boy. An a other one.' Me pointin at door. 'They are in the park. They have got a cigs an they have got my blazer.'

Cross lady gettin cross. Gettin a matches. Puttin it on counter.

Me puttin money on counter. Takin matches.

In the park. That boy tall one. He is wearin my blazer. Showin it to Bricks turnin round showin it off. Arms comin out up to a elbows showin elbows of arm. Turnin. Showin the back it is broke doin splits. Lookin at me laughin sayin: 'Im wearin your blazer.'

Me noddin.

'Do you want it back.'

Me shakin head.

'He dont even want it after all that.' Tall boy sayin it to Bricks. Tall boy lookin at me sayin: 'We was arguin about if I should wear it. Bricks reckoned you might want it back

96

an I said you probly dont even want it. We even bet on it didnt we Bricks.'

'You aint gonna bust me are you.'

'Oi lamer come ere.' Bricks gettin a way. Tall boy tellin him come ere. Bricks comin back. Tall boy grabbin holdin on a arm hittin on arm. 'A bets a bet lamer.'

'Oi.'

'I betted you fair an square he didnt want it back an he dont even want it back.'

'Only cos you busted it.'

'I didnt bust it.'

'Its got a split up the back. Oi look at the back then.'

Tall boy turnin round. Lookin at the back. Not seein it. It turnin round tall boy turnin round.

Bricks movin cig. It is in mouth the same one it is soggy. 'Oi. You get them matches.'

Me gettin em out of trouser pocket give it to Bricks.

'You can have your blazer back then.' Tall boy takin it off drop it on ground.

Me lookin at blazer. It is on park grass on a ground got split in it grass growin thru it showin thru. It is a blazer it is rubbish.

Bricks lightin cig. Lightin it up a match lightin it smokin it doin it groan up.

'Give me one of your cigs.' Tall boy sayin it to Bricks.

Bricks shakin head. Cig movin in shake shape of head. 'I aint got none.'

'Where you get that one from then.' Tall boy grabbin it have a look. Tall boy droppin it on park it is soggy. Standin on it make it go out.

Bricks lookin at cig. Bendin.

'You pick that up an I bust you.'

Bricks lookin up at tall boy. Then. Lookin down at cig it is broke. Bendin pick it up.

Tall boy punchin him on shoulder.

Bricks holdin shoulder. 'Oi now what we gonna smoke. We aint got none left. They know we aint sixteen.'

'Get him to get some.'

Bricks gettin money out of out of shape trouser pocket. Out of shape trouser pocket. Comin out of out of shape trouser gettin in side out. Bricks pushin it back in. Givin me that money sayin: 'If they wont let us buy em. They aint gonna let him buy em are they.'

'Theyll have to wont they. If he wants his tie back.' Tall boy holdin on my tie. 'Oi lamer give us that tie.' Holdin on my tie pullin it make it tight.

Bricks laughin. 'Aint you meant to be gettin it off him. Not tighten it up.'

'He can un do that carnt you lamer. If he dont he gets busted he knows that dont you lamer.' Tall boy punchin me on arm.

Bricks sayin: 'Busted.'

Tall boy punchin him on arm.

Bricks holdin arm sayin: 'Oi him I meant.'

'Well now youre both busted. Oi lamer give me that tie.'

Me tryin an un do it but. Carnt un do it.

Then.

Un doin it gettin it un done.

Next to be side sweet shop. It is a other shop a off licence for groan ups. Me in off licence askin for cigs a cigarettes. Groan up shop man gettin cross tellin me off sayin: 'You must be jokin.'

Me shakin head. Not even jokin.

Then. Door openin a man come in a other one. Man goin up to counter askin for a wine.

Me. Bendin. On zig zag purple carpet what is in shop got bits on it. Crawlin. Be hind counter. Out in back of shop.

In back of shop. It is a room like a cubberd but big it is same size of shop. It is got in it boxes piled up. Me lookin in it in box open it up.

In it. There is a packets of cigs cigarettes in it.

Me gettin one of that cigs cigarette packet put it in pocket in a back of trouser.

Then.

Crawlin. In shop be hind counter. On zig zag carpet. Lookin up at man. Man. Talkin to other man customer man. Got a wine put it in bag.

Customer man openin door. Me crawlin under legs. Standin runnin out of shop runnin round back of shops.

In the park. When I get back in it. That boy tall one an other one Bricks. They aint even in it.

There is other big boys standin playin on slide. Me goin up to em sayin: 'Where is that tall boy.'

Big boys not sayin.

Me goin up to big boy standin on slide on top. Lookin up at big boy. Sayin: 'Where is that tall boy.'

Big boy not sayin nothin. Slidin down slide.

Me walkin round slide goin round to ladder what a big boy is standin on. Holdin on trouser leg pullin it pullin his leg.

Big boy lookin down. 'What you doin.'

'That boy,' I say sayin it what I am doin. 'I am askin it. Where he is.'

'What boy.'

'Tall one.' Me holdin up hand doin shape of tall. 'An other one Bricks. They made me go a shop get a cigs.' Me holdin out cigs. 'They was over there but. They aint even there.' Pointin at where they aint there.

'Yeah they had to go home.'

Other big boy sayin: 'They said you have to give em to us lot.'

'O,' I say givin em em. 'But. He is got my tie.'

Big boy openin the cig cigarette packet. Takin out it a cig. Put it in mouth.

'He is got my tie,' I say. 'He—'

Big boy shruggin. Givin cig packet to other big boy. Other big boy. Takin out it a cig. Put it in mouth.

Me sayin: 'It—'

Big boy shruggin.

Me standin ere look at big boys what are shruggin. Cigs in mouth movin up an down doin cig shrug aint even got a light.

Me walkin on park goin over there at a other end of park.

Then. When I am goin out of park out of gate park gate. There is that boys. Tall one turnin lookin at me sayin: 'You get em.'

Bricks sayin: 'Oi did he get em.'

'I gave em to that boys,' I say pointin at park.

Tall boy lookin at park. At big boys at other end of park. 'Oi what you give em to them lamers for.'

'They told me to give em to em,' I say sayin it.

'If you dont bust him for that.' Bricks sayin: 'You aint never gonna bust him.'

Tall boy punchin me on arm. 'Busted.'

'Ow.'

Bricks laughin.

'Oi what you laughin for. Some lamers con us out of our cigs an youre laughin.' Tall boy punchin Bricks on arm. 'You should be bustin em not laughin.'

'I will bust em.'

'Can I have my tie back.'

Tall boy takin it out of trouser pocket rolled up. 'Well bust em then.'

'I will bust em.'

'Then go an bust em.'

Me lookin at tie.

Bricks lookin at big boys. 'Theres eight of em.'

'Then bust eight of em.'

'I carnt bust eight of em.'

Tall boy puttin tie back in pocket pushin it in. 'Look wait ere.' Puttin hand on gate park gate. Goin in park. Walkin. On that park. Gettin small gettin at other end of park.

Me an Bricks watchin.

Bricks noddin head sayin: 'Hes gonna bust em.'

Me noddin.

Tall boy gettin at other end of park at slide. Goin up to one of that big boys. Big boy shruggin. Tall boy gettin cigs punchin him on a arm.

Bricks lookin at me sayin: 'He busted em.'

Me noddin.

Me an Bricks lookin at Bricks an me lookin at each other. Smilin. Laughin.

Me an Bricks an tall boy sittin on wall. It is brick wall at front of school. Bricks sittin on it on brick wall climbin up on it sittin on it on brick wall. Tall boy holdin on Bricks pullin his shoe off throwin it over wall. Bricks sayin: Oi me shoe you chucked it. Tall boy laughin. Pullin him off wall.

Bricks fallin on concrete out side school. Tall boy sittin on Bricks. Punchin Bricks on arm sayin: Busted. Bricks sayin: Get off. Tall boy shakin head. Sayin: Shut it lamer. Bricks sayin: Oi get off. Tall boy gettin off. Bricks standin up. Climbin up on wall sittin on brick wall. Tall boy climbin up on wall on brick wall. Then. Sittin. On Bricks. On brick wall. Punchin him on arm sayin: Busted. Bricks sayin: Ow. Tall boy gettin off fallin off. Bricks gettin off jumpin off. Landin on tall boy. Laughin. Tall boy pushin him off grabbin him throwin him over wall.

Me an tall boy laughin. On a own. There aint even a Bricks.

Then.

Climbin up on wall. Bricks. Laughin. Holdin shoe sayin: I found it me shoe.

Me an Bricks an tall boy talkin to a girls. They are girls at school Big School. It is after school girls comin out of school me an Bricks an tall boy waitin for girls watchin em come out. Bricks sayin: I got a stiffy. Tall boy tellin him to shut up. Bricks shuttin up. Then. Two of girls come over tall boy callin em over.

Tall boy sayin: 'Oi where we gonna do it then.'

Bricks laughin.

Girls standin got arms folded on front of chest hidin it what they got.

Bricks sayin: 'Oi. What about—'

Tall boy punchin him on arm.

'Oi what you bustin me for.'

'I felt like it.'

One of girls smilin. Foldin arms.

Tall boy sayin: 'Come on Bricks out with it.'

'Oi forgot what I was sayin now. Oi yeah.' Bricks memberin it what he is sayin. Sayin it what he is sayin. 'You know that mole kid. Oi find that mole kid.' Bricks walkin off lookin for that kid.

Tall boy shakin head.

One of girls foldin a arms. 'Whats he on about.'

Bricks walkin round play ground lookin at boys. Findin one of boys. Puttin arm round shoulder havin a word.

That boy. He is like a mole he is little like a mole. Bigger than me but littler than Bricks an tall boy an like a mole.

Me an tall boy an that girls goin over to that boy that kid that mole kid.

Bricks sayin: 'He knows where that house is.'

Mole kid noddin.

'Its a house what aint lived in. Him an his brother made a camp in it.'

Tall boy shakin head. 'Oi whats the point makin a camp in a house for. If youve got a house. You dont need a camp.'

'Oi yeah but it stinks though. You have to wear nose plugs or somethin aint that right.'

Mole kid noddin. Openin bag. It is school bag it is got in it. Books. Pee ee kit. Pencil case shape like a mole it is a animal. Openin pencil case showin it. It. What is in it.

Tall boy sayin: 'What are they.'

Mole kid gettin one out. Puttin it up nose up a nose nozzle nostle.

Tall boy noddin.

Mole kid sniffin. Droppin it out nose catchin it.

Tall boy punchin Bricks on arm. 'Busted.'

Me an tall boy an Bricks an that mole kid an that girls. Walkin. Goin round house of that mole kid. Mole kid sayin:

'You have to get in round the back. Its round the back. The house is round the back of my house. Their garden. Their back garden.'

Mole kid openin door of house. It is front door it is house what that mole kid lives in. Openin door puttin in it a key gettin it out mole skin trouser puttin it in key hole in door.

'Oi.' Bricks hittin mole kid on back. 'Oi lamer is your mum in.'

Mole kid shakin head.

'Oi oi oi.' Bricks sayin: 'Can I wank off in your mums bed.'

Girls foldin arms.

Tall boy punchin Bricks on arm.

Bricks holdin arm sayin: 'Oi what you bust me for.'

'Thats what you get. For callin him a lamer.'

'He is a lamer.'

'Oi not when youre goin round his house. Oi youre the lamer you lamer.' Tall boy punchin Bricks on arm.

Bricks noddin. Holdin arm.

Girls foldin a arms.

Mole kid openin door front door goin in. In the house it is a door mat got a picture on it of a mole. It says: Mole sweet mole. Mole kid lookin at tall boy sayin: 'My mum likes moles.'

Bricks sayin: 'Oi does she like you then.'

Mole kid noddin.

Bricks lookin up at tall boy. Laughin.

Tall boy laughin.

Every one goin in. Goin in front room. Front door shuttin some one shuttin it.

Tall boy turnin on telly. Sittin on arm chair. Watchin telly.

'Oi.' Bricks sayin it to mole kid sayin: 'Can I have a drink.'

Me an mole kid an Bricks goin in kitchen. That mole kid. He has got a lot of difrent kitchen stuff. He is got. Internet oven. Jelly wobble maker. Micro wave fridge.

Bricks sayin: 'Oi lamer whats this.'

'My mum bought it for my birthday. Molecule modifier. It turns carrots in to sweets.' Mole kid openin cubberd gettin out it a carrot. Open lid of molecule modifier. Put it in it. Put on lid on it. Press a button program it. Then. It openin at bottom carrot shape sweets come out.

Bricks laughin. Eatin that carrot shape sweets.

Me gettin a sweet eat it.

Bricks goin in front room. 'Oi look at what that mole kids got.'

Tall boy standin up. 'Oi lamer this better be good.'

Me an mole kid an Bricks an tall boy an girl an me an a other girl. In kitchen. Mole kid showin that molecule modifier. Makin a carrots in to a sweets. Open lid of molecule modifier. Put it in it. Put on it a lid. Press a button program it. Then. It openin at bottom carrot shape sweets come out.

Tall boy sayin: 'Oi put somethin else in.'

'It only works with food.' Mole kid sayin: 'Vegetables.'

Bricks sayin: 'Oi put one of them cigs in.'

Tall boy gettin out a cig. Givin it to mole kid. Mole kid open lid of molecule modifier. Put it in it a cig a cigarettes. Put on lid on it. Press a button program it. Then. It openin at bottom it comin out a sweet flavour sweet cigarettes.

Bricks laughin.

Tall boy sayin: 'Busted.'

Bricks eatin it that sweet cigarettes. 'Oi put somethin else in.'

'Oi this tie.' Tall boy got it in pocket of trousers. It rolled up un roll it put it in molecule modifier. Put lid on it. Press a button program it. Then. It openin at bottom it comin out a tie made of sweets. Tall boy takin tie tyin it up puttin it on wearin it. 'Oi I hate wearin a tie but this ones bustin.'

Bricks laughin. Bendin down suckin it bottom of it pointy bit.

Tall boy punchin him on arm.

Bricks movin out of way. Tie made of sweets in his mouth it gettin broke off snappin off.

'Oi you busted it you lamer.' Tall boy hittin Bricks on arm.

Bricks chokin he is got it in his mouth that tie made of sweets. Bendin over doin coughin it up.

Tall boy puttin arm round Bricks lookin at girls sayin: 'Oi quick get him some cough mixture.'

Girl lookin at other girl.

Other girl. Lookin at mole kid. Sayin: 'Excuse me have you got some cough mixture.'

Bricks doin coughin.

Mole kid goin in corner of kitchen. Openin cubberd. Gettin out it a box it is plastic made red. Open lid get out it a things what are in it. Put it on work top countin it.

Me lookin at what it is. It is. Plasters. Bandage. Head ache tablets. Put it in your head it is got a ache.

Bricks doin coughin.

Tall boy sayin: 'Oi hurry up you lamer. Hes coughin his guts up.'

Mole kid findin it. It is a cough mixture shakin bottle takin off it a lid. Tall boy takin bottle put it in Bricks in his mouth tippin it.

Bricks swallowin it that cough mixture. Not even coughin.

Tall boy sayin: 'Oi. Oi you alright now lamer.'

Girl sayin: 'Are you alright.'

Bricks noddin head it is red.

Tall boy noddin. 'Nice one. Oi a jokes a joke yeah.'

Bricks noddin.

'Oi.' Tall boy sayin: 'Shall we go round that house that camp.'

Bricks noddin.

Girls foldin a arms.

Every one open back door goin out in garden. Mole kid an tall boy an Bricks an that girls.

Then. Out in garden. One of girls sayin it to tall boy sayin: 'Where did that little boy go.'

'What that little kid.'

Tall boy comin back in. Lookin in kitchen. Lookin in front room. At arm chair at that Tom. 'Oi. Oi whats a matter.'

Bricks comin in sayin: 'Did you bust him.'

'Oi. You dont bust some little kid if hes cryin.' Tall boy hittin Bricks on arm.

Bricks holdin on a arm. 'Oi I meant is that what hes cryin for. Cos you busted him.'

'I never busted him.'

'Oi what about in the park.'

Girl sayin: 'Is that why youre cryin.'

Me shakin head.

'Oi every one get out.' Tall boy gettin every one goin out. Goin in kitchen muck a bout.

Girl puttin arms round sayin: 'Has some one said somethin. Theyre only muckin about you know.'

In that garden of mole kid. It has got a grass green cut neat. Then. In it in that grass. There is a mud mound piled up on grass. Tall boy kickin mud mound piled up sayin: 'Oi what are these for.'

Mole kid sayin: 'Mole hills.'

Tall boy laughin.

Bricks laughin. 'Oi did you make em.'

Mole kid shakin head.

Tall boy diggin it in it a shoe. 'Oi get it to come up ere then we can bust em for bustin his lawn.'

Bricks laughin.

Tall boy diggin it muckin a bout.

Mole kid at back of garden. Got a open in fence a broke bit open it up. Mole kid goin in that hole in fence.

Tall boy goin in that hole bendin he is tall.

Bricks goin in.

Girls gettin me goin in it make sure I am alright.

Then. Girls goin in it shuttin it foldin a arms.

Every one in a other garden at back of back garden. It is got grass in it tall up to top of head of Tom. Makin that Tom get lost in it. Girls findin it laughin foldin a arms.

Mole kid walkin thru grass at front of back garden at back of house. Open a door aint even locked it is broke mole kid an mole kids brother broked it goin in it makin in it a camp.

Tall boy lookin in door. Tall boy holdin a nose sayin: 'Shit.'

Mole kid shuttin door. Openin school bag it is got in it. Torch. Plasters. Pack lunch. Fizzy drink. Mole kid puttin it in it in kitchen gettin ready. Pencil case shape like mole. Mole kid openin it gettin out a nose plugs.

Hold out a hand. Mole kid put it in it a nose plugs.

Tall boy puttin it up nose nozzle nostle one up each one. 'Oi Im goin first.' Sayin it funny nose plugs makin it funny. Goin in comin out sayin: 'Shit.'

Bricks puttin nose plugs up nose nozzle nostle.

Mole kid puttin it up nose nozzle nostle.

Girls puttin it up pretty girl nose. Helpin that Tom that little kid put it up nose nozzle nostle.

Mole kid gettin out torch zip up school bag turn it on. Point it at house. Goin in.

Tall boy puttin hand on door frame side holdin on it goin in.

Bricks goin in.

Me an that girls. Not goin in.

Tall boy takin torch off mole kid. 'Oi lamer is that all rubbish.'

Mole kid noddin.

'Didnt they never throw nothin away.'

Mole kid shakin head.

'Thats what all the stink is then. Oi lamer they comin in or what.'

Bricks lookin out door. 'Are you lot comin in or what.'

Girls foldin arms.

Me an girls goin in shuttin door puttin hand on shoulder. Doin a look after.

Tall boy shinin torch round room. Shinin it on rubbish bin bags of rubbish. 'Oi wheres this camp then.'

Tall boy givin torch to mole kid.

Mole kid got torch walkin thru rubbish bin bags of rubbish. Shinin it on wood wall findin it. 'The camp.' It is a wood wall made of wood. It is got in it a door made of wood. Mole kid openin it. Goin in it.

Every one goin in it goin in wood door. Goin in shuttin door. Mole kid shuttin it shuttin out that stink. Takin out that nose plugs. Sniffin it in hand.

Tall boy takin out nose plugs. 'Oi. Oi you can take em out. How come you can take em out.'

Mole kid shinin torch at ceiling roof made of wood. It is got on it. Air freshners. It is hundreds of em pink an green stuck on ceiling roof up side down. Then. Mole kid shinin torch at corner at pipe. 'Washing machine pipe. My brother. It goes out side.'

Tall boy noddin.

Bricks takin out nose plugs. Hold out hand sniff em in to hand.

Mole kid turnin on light. It is in corner on floor a plastic one goin camping. Mole kid turnin it on lightin up wood room camp. 'We sealed it at the edges.' Mole kid showin it pointin at edges. It is got tape on it sticky tape on edges joinin it up.

'Oi when you gonna do it then.' Bricks sayin it to tall boy.

Girl foldin arms. 'I aint doin it in ere. Its my first time. I want it to be special.'

Tall boy sayin: 'So theres no point comin ere then.'

Mole kid lookin at floor.

Bricks sayin: 'Oi what if we jus wank off—'

Tall boy hittin Bricks on arm.

Bricks holdin arm.

Girl foldin a arm. 'Id do it on the bed. In the bed room.'

'Yeah lets do it up there.' Bricks sayin: 'It might be alright up there.'

'Lamer you aint gettin any any way so I dont know what youre worried about.'

Bricks shruggin.

Girl sayin: 'It might be alright up there. There might not be any up there.'

Mole kid lookin up. Lookin at tall boy. 'My brother. We didnt go up stairs.'

'Oi lamer.' Tall boy sayin it to Bricks sayin: 'How a bout me an you go up there. Have a nose.'

Bricks noddin.

Mole kid openin door.

Every one holdin a nose.

Tall boy an Bricks puttin nose plugs in a nose nozzle nostle. Goin out door.

Bricks sayin it funny nose noise sayin: 'Oi. Oi bring that little kid.'

Tall boy sayin: 'Have you got your nose plugs. Put your nose plugs in.'

Me puttin em in.

Me shinin torch on bags. Tall boy an Bricks movin bags. Holdin a nose movin bags makin noise. Stink makin em make noise. Even got that nose plugs it stinks. Throwin bags on a arm chair got on it rubbish come out of bags makin it stink.

Then. Openin door.

Tall boy got torch shinin it out it. Out in hall. Shinin it on front door. Not openin it. Not goin out. 'Oi thats the way out yeah. If anythin happens.'

Bricks noddin. Holdin on my arm makin sure I am alright. Makin me come out in hall.

Tall boy shinin torch up stairs. It is up stairs like—

Me lookin at front door. Lookin up stairs.

Tall boy goin up stairs. Bricks goin up stairs. Me holdin on to Bricks goin up stairs gettin scared.

Tall boy gettin at top of stairs. Holdin on stairs wall side. Shinin torch on in room. 'Bath room. Oi this is the bed rooms.' Shinin torch on bed room door of bed room. Goin in bed room like in bed room in my house. Openin door goin in.

Me an Bricks goin in. In bed room of my house. Me sayin: 'Its my house.'

Tall boy lookin at me. 'Oi shut up. Youre givin me the creeps.'

Me holdin on to Bricks. Holdin on to tall boy.

'It carnt be your house no one lives ere.'

'It is my house.' Me sayin it quiet. 'What I lived in. It is my room.'

Tall boy noddin. 'Oi if you say so.' Tall boy shinin torch on rubbish bin bags of rubbish on bed. On shelfs. On fishes made of paper cut out hung up.

'Oi busted.' Bricks says: 'Oi turn the light on.'

'You carnt you lamer they been cut off.'

Me turnin light on.

Light. Comin on.

Tall boy lookin at me. Bricks lookin at me.

'Oi how did you do that.' Tall boy sayin: 'How did you know where the light switch is.'

'Its my room. I know it. Where it is.'

'The lights work.' Tall boy laughin. 'Oi that mole kid dont know what hes talkin a bout.'

Bricks openin cubberd gettin out it a toys. 'Oi we could sell all this.'

Me lookin at toys.

Tall boy pushin rubbish bin bags of rubbish off bed gettin on bed. 'Oi get her to come up ere. Oi lamer help me turn this mattress over.'

Me lookin at bed. At bear. 'It is my room. Look. Thats my bear.'

'That aint your bear.'

'It is.'

Tall boy lookin at bear. 'Oi. Whats his name then.'

Bricks laughin. 'Oi dont he might start cryin again. Oi. Oi thats how to prove it aint his room.'

Me tryin an takin bear. 'Its mine,' I say not even cryin. 'Its Poll Tax Clown my bear.'

'Poll Tax Clown.' Tall boy laughin. 'It aint a clown if its a bear is it.'

Bricks sayin: 'Cut his eyes like crosses like a clown.'

Tall boy laughin. Gettin out a knife a pen knife it aint even a pen. Gettin it out. Puttin bear on bed. Puttin tall knee on bear. Cuttin up a eye.

Me tryin an take it.

Tall boy not lettin me take it. Cuttin up a eye a other one.

'Its mine.' Me tryin an take it.

Tall boy not lettin me take it.

Bricks holdin my arms. Holdin on back of arms. 'Oi cut his arms off.'

'Dont,' I say. 'Dont cut my arms off.'

'Not your arms you lamer.'

Tall boy laughin. Cuttin that bear.

Bricks holdin my arms.

'Right. Let him go. If he touches that bear. We bust him.'

Bricks lettin go my arms.

Me lookin rubbin arms. Lookin at bear. It is on bed. It is Poll Tax Clown. It is a bear but. It is got eyes cut up like crossed eyed clown eyes. It is got. It is got his arms cut off an put on up side down like he is hold his arm holders his shoulders.

Tall boy laughin.

Bricks lookin at eyes. 'He aint cryin that means it aint his bear.'

'I know it aint his bear. Oi this mattress stinks. Oi lamer check the other bed room.'

'I aint goin in there. You go in there.'

'Get in there or I bust you.'

'You can bust me.' Bricks sayin: 'I aint goin in no more rooms.'

Tall boy hittin Bricks on arm.

Bricks rubbin arm. Not goin in.

'Oi give us them nose plugs.' Tall boy tryin an take that nose plugs out nose nozzle nostle of that Bricks.

'Oi.'

Bricks goin out on landin tall boy pushin him out on landin. Bricks holdin nose. Tall boy punchin arm makin him not hold nose. Bricks holdin arm holdin nose. Tall boy punchin other arm makin him not hold nose. Tall boy openin door of other bed room my mums bed room got in it her dresses they are gone. Punchin Bricks on arm. 'Oi get in there.' Pushin Bricks in. Bricks comin out. Tall boy punchin Bricks on arm. Pushin him in. Shuttin door not let him get out.

Tall boy listenin at door.

Me an tall boy listenin at door.

Handle movin door Bricks tryin open it.

Tall boy laughin. Holdin handle not let it open.

Me an tall boy listenin. Bricks sayin: 'Oi its the worst smell. Oi wheres the light.' Light comin on it comin out of under a door.

Then.

Bricks screamin.

Bricks screamin tryin turn handle open door.

Bricks hittin door.

Bricks screamin hittin door.

Handle movin tall boy holdin it not let it open. Laughin.

Bricks screamin kickin door screamin shoutin tryin make a words but carnt make a words.

Tall boy lookin at me. Not laughin.

Bricks shoutin screamin kickin door hittin door hittin head on door.

Tall boy lookin at me. Lookin at door let it open.

Bricks standin at door bein sick.

Bricks comin out door runnin down stairs fallin over bein sick.

Tall boy goin in room.

Tall boy bein sick. Comin out of room. Goin down stairs.

Me goin in room. Look at it at what is in it.

There is a dead boy here.

He is my age he is goes to my school he is me a boy.

He is got—

He has got his arms cut off an put up side down like he is hold his arm holders his shoulders.

He is got his eyes cut up.

Me goin out of room.

Down stairs. Me goin down stairs. Shut door of mums room it is a worst smell. Shut door. Goin down stairs.

Front door open every one gone out it. It is the way out. If anythin happens.

In front room. Light is on me put it on wave at it say hello. It is my front room what I lived in. It is got chair arm chair what I sitted on watch telly. It is got rubbish bin bags of rubbish. It is got table made of a camp what I sat up doin colourin in eat your dinner. It is put in front room made a camp. Got bits of wood an other bit of wood. Make it a camp. The mole kid an that mole kids brother. Got a door it is open a light in it goin camping.

Me goin up stairs. Hold a nose. Got in it a nose plugs in nose nozzle nostle. Hold a nose it is got a smell in it a boy what is cut up. Me goin up stairs.

Boxford

It is my bear I got it. It—

It is broked.

I am Tom I am out side a place a play place a theatre. It is a theatre where they do plays.

Me lookin up at play place. It is a theatre got on it lights shinin bright make it look nice. Me sittin out side it lookin up at that lights.

Me lookin over road. It is a building a side of it. On it it is a sign sayin: Lester Square.

It is night time it is dark but it aint that dark there is that lights. There is a lot of people doin walkin doin it fast. Me lookin up at legs walkin past I am little.

Next to be side me. There is a man doin sleepin.

There aint a dead boy.

Me sittin.

Then. Jus when I am sittin. A door open me movin out

of way a man comin out two of em carryin a box it is big. On it it says: Costumes.

Me lookin in where they are come out of.

It is a play place a theatre. It is back stage at back of stage. It is where they make that play put it in theatre. Door shuttin man an other man puttin box in lorry goin in back in theatre shuttin door. Lorry drivin off. On it it says: Costumes & Props London.

Me sittin. Closin a eyes. Goin a sleep.

It is easy goin a sleep is. Even if you aint got a bed it is easy. Me gettin Poll Tax Clown off bed puttin bear arms in pocket of school trouser Prim bought an other one in other one. Goin out of house holdin bear middle an topper bear head it is got legs. Doin walk doin it all day an a night an a other day an a other night. Goin in shop get a food put it in pocket an tum goin out side eat it get told off. Doin sleep in park an shop alley door way. Then. Doin it out side theatre.

It is easy goin a sleep is but it aint easy at a theatre. Jus when I am goin a sleep. Door openin me movin out of way man comin out two of em carryin a box it is big. On it it says: Props.

Me lookin in it where they come out.

Then.

Goin in. Doin it quick goin in.

Me an Poll Tax Clown in back of theatre. Bear middle an topper an bear legs holdin in arms doin hug a bear hug.

It is spring but it is night time it aint spring at night time. It is cold me gettin cold goin in theatre in doors goin in door.

Me an Poll Tax Clown in back of theatre. Gettin lost in

it goin in it smellin that wood. It is smell of wood damp got rot. Under it that floor boards up a stairs it is dark. Then. Findin it. A curtain.

Me liftin curtain. It is heavy me liftin it a bit goin under it have a look.

Me on stage at back of stage lookin at what is on it. On it it has got. Carpet rug. Chairs. Arm chairs got a arm on it some one sit on it put on it a arm. A lamp shade light shade. A sofa a settee.

Me crawlin under curtain be hind sofa settee. Standin up have a look.

It is a man doin talk a play. A man a lady doin talk. It is a audience watchin it that play.

Man stoppin talkin. Lookin. At me.

Audience lookin. At me.

No one doin nothin.

Then.

Me holdin up bear topper head part. Holdin it up. Every one laughin lookin at me that bear.

Back stage theatre man not laughin. He is a back stage man runnin on stage holdin me on arm tellin me off gettin me off stage.

Me in audience watchin play. Theatre man puttin me in audience. Keepin a eye on me. Where he can keep an eye on me.

In the play. It is a mum an dad havin a talk. Mum sayin: 'I hope Tim has a good day at school today.'

Dad noddin. Readin a noose paper it is big.

Mum sayin: 'I did the ironing today.' Holdin up a ironing a basket got in it clobes neat ones folded up. Mum holdin up jeans neat ones folded up. Jeans un foldin with the holdin. Holdin em up sayin: 'I ironed Tims jeans.'

Dad puttin down noose paper. Foldin it up. Puttin it on sofa settee. Standin up. Lookin at jeans.

'These are his best jeans.' Mum sayin: 'He can wear them on Sunday when we visit Gran and Grandad.'

Dad noddin. Pickin up noose paper. Un foldin it holdin it up. It un foldin with the holdin. Sittin on sofa settee. Readin noose paper.

'What are you reading about dear.'

'It says here. That things are getting better.'

Mum doin a sigh. 'Thats one less thing to worry about.'

'O you musnt worry dear.'

'My only worry.' Mum says: 'Is that Tim gets a good education.'

'He will get a good education. Hes at Norris Apprehensive Comprehensive.'

Mum noddin.

Dad turnin page of noose paper. Readin noose paper. 'It says here. That Norris is top of the school league table. Also that Tim is top of the class.'

'Thats good.'

'And it says here. That the head teacher has been cleared of all charges.'

Mum noddin. Foldin jeans put em in iron basket. Lookin at clock. 'Its nearly time for Tim to come home.'

Dad noddin.

Then. A sound a door knock knockin a knocker. Mum goin off stage off that side goin back stage. Comin back on stage. Tim comin on stage. He is a boy he is my age but. On stage. Sayin: 'Hello Dad.'

'Hello Tim.' Dad sayin: 'How was school today.'

'It was great.'

'Did any one get told off.'

'No.' Tim says: 'No one gets told off at Norris. If you do something bad. They give you a hug and take you to the Talk It Thru room.'

Dad noddin. Foldin noose paper. 'And what happens there.'

'I dont know.' Tim sittin next to be side Dad on sofa settee. 'No one has ever had to go in there.'

Dad noddin.

Mum noddin. Pattin Tim on head.

'I love it at Norris.' Tim says: 'Every one is so well adjusted.'

'Tim.' Mum says: 'Daddy has an announcement to make. Havent you Daddy.'

Dad standin up. 'Yes. I have a new job.'

Tim lookin up at Dad. Doin it wide eyed.

'Im not going to be a business man any more. I have a new job. An exciting new job.'

'What is it Daddy.'

'You have to guess.'

Mum sayin: 'Show him the uniform.'

Dad got a bag. Holdin it up. Gettin out a patch a eye patch it is black. Put it on a eye.

Tim lookin con fuse.

Mum sayin: 'Show him the hat.'

Dad openin bag gettin out it a hat a black hat funny shape. Put it on head.

Tim lookin at hat. Lookin con fuse.

'What about the wooden leg.' Mum sayin: 'Show him the wooden leg.'

Dad goin be hind sofa settee sofa. It is that one what I went be hind hidin be hind it standin up. Dad gettin a wooden leg holdin it up. Bendin knee puttin knee on wooden leg top. Doin a walk got a wooden leg sayin: 'Shiver me timbers.'

Tim lookin con fuse.

Dad openin bag get out it a hook hold it in hand a hook hand hook. Gettin a parrot gettin bird poo on shoulder put it on shoulder. Gettin out a flag.

Mum sayin: 'The flag will give it away. Dont you think Daddy.'

Dad sayin: 'Yes he will get it when he sees the flag.'

Tim lookin con fuse. Lookin at flag.

Dad holdin up that flag wavin it a flag. It is black it is got on it. A skelly ton skull an cross bones it is cross. Dad wavin it not gettin cross Tim not gettin told off.

Tim smilin jumpin up an down sayin: 'O I know. Youre going to be. A pirate.'

Dad noddin.

Tim goin to front of stage lookin at audience. 'My dad is a pirate. Sailing the seven seas. Shooting baddies with a cannon. And digging for buried treasure.'

Audience laughin.

Me standin up. Standin on chair lookin round at that audience. They are laughin it is a dad a pirate.

'Some dads.' Tim says: 'Take drugs and go to prison. But not my dad. My dad is the best dad. In the whole wide world.'

An that is it. A end.

Every one standin up. It is a end of play. Every one goin out of theatre. Every one in audience goin out of audience sayin: Yes it was good yes. Did you enjoy it. Yes it was good rather. Fine performances all round. Goin out of theatre up steps goin out.

Me not goin out.

Lights comin on it aint even dark.

121

Back stage theatre man comin out of in door door. Tellin me off sayin: 'Are you still here. Where are your parents.'

'I aint got one,' I say sayin it. 'My mum. She—'

'Yes.'

'My dad is a pirate.'

Back stage theatre man laughin.

'He is sailin a seven seas.'

Back stage theatre man noddin head. Laughin.

Then. Boy my age on stage comin off stage. Comin out of curtain lookin at theatre there aint no one there aint a audience. Boy comin off stage walkin down steps. Walkin past. Then. Seein me comin back sayin: 'Youre the little sod who stormed the stage.'

He is a little kid but. He is callin me little.

'You could have brought the house down. You could have ruined the entire performance.'

Me shruggin.

'You attention seeking little sod. Why are you still here. Why havent they fed you to the lions. And whats that.'

Me lookin at Poll Tax Clown got it in arms holdin it.

'What is it.' Boy takin it holdin its head it aint got a arms. Boy holdin it up lookin at it turnin it over lookin it over. 'Now it looks like it used to be a teddy bear. Once upon a time. In a former life. Before some kind soul took a hack saw to it. And put it out of its misery. What happened to the eyes.'

'It—'

'And where are the arms.'

Me got em in pocket in trouser.

'Why not ask your mother to mend it. Or better still. Sling it out. And buy you another.'

'My—'

'Dont tell me.' Boy got hand on hip holdin bear. 'They carnt afford to. Your parents are inner city. Which raises the question. Of why you were allowed to enter my fathers theatre in the first place.'

Me lookin at back stage theatre man.

Back stage theatre man not sayin nothin.

Me lookin at boy. 'I—'

'Please dont tell me youre with that disgusting school party. Why they let a bunch of school children in to a theatre I do not know. Inner city children at that.'

Me not sayin nothin.

'Right here come my parents.'

Me bitin lip.

'My father.' Boy pointin. 'Who you will not have heard of. Him being neither foot baller nor film star. My father. Who does actually own this theatre. And who does not tolerate moronity on any level. And will I am in absolutely no doubt. Have you fed to the lions. My father.' Boy foldin arms. 'Do you know who he is. Have you any idea. My father. Is Lord Hamilton Mild. My father owns this theatre. Which means. You know what I am about to say dont you.' Boy pointin at roof. 'Which means that my father owns every living breathing soul under this roof.'

Me not sayin nothin.

Boy not sayin nothin. Makin face.

There is a foot step shoe sound it is a parents walkin down stairs be tween chair seats of theatre.

No one sayin nothin.

Parents walkin comin over.

'Mother. Father.'

'Oscar what are you playing at.' Father sayin: 'Whos your little friend.'

123

'O just some little terrorist. A bear toting maniac with no agenda. Dont worry I have grilled him.'

Theatre back stage man sayin: 'Lord Hamilton this young man has become separated from his parents.' Lookin at watch sayin: 'I have to pop over to Lord Busbys for a bottle of sparkle with Lord Fizz. Will you keep an eye on him. I shall remain in contact with reception. And inform you of any news.'

'Quite.' Lord Hamilton noddin. 'You can mail me on my virtual mobile.' Lord Hamilton holdin up fone it is in visible he aint even got it. 'Mean time.' Lord Hamilton lookin at me. 'Whats your name.'

'Tom,' I say sayin it not gettin told off not gettin fed to a lions.

'Tom whom.'

'Boler.'

'Tom Boler. Well Tom Boler this is Lady Eliza Mild. My good lady wife.'

Lady Eliza Mild holdin out hand got on it a gold ring finger pearl neck lace brace let. Holdin my hand doin it posh sayin: 'Tom how do you do.'

Me sayin: 'How do you.'

'And my son Oscar Mild whom you have met.'

Oscar Mild makin a face.

'Oscar is the greatest actor of his size stature and shoe size of his generation. Graduated from the Precocia School aged just four and a half. With full honours. Oscar.' Lord Hamilton sayin: 'Grant us a flourish.'

Oscar noddin. Steppin back goin over there. Holdin out a hand doin a flourish. Makin it make shape of flower fallin off flower tree. Turnin it over that hand. Bendin over. Puttin out a foot shoe. Holdin it. Then. Standin up bendin head it is a flourish it is finish.

Lord Hamilton clappin hands.

Lady Eliza clappin hands.

Back stage theatre man winkin at me clappin hands.

Me lookin at Oscar Mild. Clappin hands.

Lord Hamilton goin out of theatre. Steppin out standin on pavement. Lookin up at sky holdin out hand like it is rainin but it aint. Holdin out hand lookin at sky sayin: 'Yes. It is night time. Just as I suspected.'

Lady Eliza noddin. Holdin a Lord Hamilton arm.

'Look.' Lord Hamilton pointin at sky sayin: 'Stars. If you look closely. And squint. They may just spell your name.'

Lady Eliza lookin up at sky at that stars.

Me standin next to be side Lord Hamilton. Lookin up at stars.

Oscar Mild look at man in street in gutter.

'Come.' Lord Hamilton says: 'Dinner.'

Lord Hamilton an Lady Eliza walkin off up pavement posh shoes on pavement makin posh noise.

Oscar Mild walkin up to man in street in gutter. He is got coat on got dirt water on it he is in shop window door way gettin out the way goin a sleep. Oscar Mild givin him a kick doin it little he is little.

Man not sayin nothin.

Oscar Mild smilin at man sayin: 'You want some money I suppose.'

Man not sayin nothin.

'Do you accept credit gun.' Oscar Mild gettin out a gun a toy. It is a credit gun shoots money numbers in a laser. 'Shall I credit your account. Whom shall I make it payable to.' Pointin gun at man it aint even credit gun it is a toy. 'You people make me sick. Have you any idea. How irritating it is. To walk the streets. Paved with chewing gum as they are. Only to be stopped every fifty yards by a heroin head such as your self.' Oscar Mild puttin hand in pocket takin it out turn it in side out. 'Do you know what this is. Do you see.'

Man not sayin nothin.

'Have you any idea.' Oscar Mild pointin at theatre we come out it goin out side it that door. 'In your small mind. Have you absolutely any idea. How much a place like that costs to run. My father spends millions per head per year on gold rimmed pamphlets alone. The toilets in this building are two hundred years old older than the building itself.' Oscar Mild puttin hands on hips doin a step. 'Now if you think that means we have money to burn then you are clinically moronic. Capital yes. Liquid assets no. It is all on the plastic. Some of it is digital but that is virtual and none of your business. Some of it is on graph paper. That man there.' Oscar Mild pointin at Lord Hamilton walkin stopped turnin holdin a arm. 'Have you any idea. How much that man is worth.'

Man not sayin nothin. Not even shakin head.

'That man is my father. And let me tell you something else. That man.' Oscar Mild pointin at Lord Hamilton. 'If my father catches you pestering me for money again. He will have you fed to the lions. Do I make my self clear.'

Man not sayin nothin. Not makin a self clear.

Oscar Mild kickin man on head.

'Fuck off.'

'Do I make my self clear.'

Lord Hamilton turnin lookin at a Oscar.

Lady Eliza lettin go a arm comin over walkin got posh frock sayin: 'Oscar those shoes were brand new this morning dont get shit on them theres a dear. Now come along.'

'I can in fact hold my own.' Oscar Mild lookin at man. Oscar Mild sayin: 'With out even putting my hands in to my trouser pockets.'

Lord Hamilton openin door. Holdin open a door.

Oscar Mild goin in goin under a arm.

Me goin in goin under a arm. Lookin at door.

Lady Eliza goin in.

Lord Hamilton goin in. Shuttin door.

Out side it. It aint even a eat place. It is got windows shut up shop it aint even got nothin on it. Then. In side it. It is a eat place a restaurant it is posh. It is little got two tables it aint got a other ones. One of em is little got a man black an big sat eat on a own. Other table is big one. Restaurant lady comin out showin that table. Every one sat round table. Restaurant lady got menu book give you it. Every one look at it Lord Hamilton sayin: 'Oscar.'

Oscar lookin at menu book. 'I will have. The squid on the ranch.'

Lord Hamilton sayin: 'Tom.'

Me lookin at menu book. Not sayin nothin.

Oscar sayin: 'Just get him some pudding. Mother what are you having.'

Lady Eliza lookin at menu book. 'I shall have. The goat on the prairie.'

'And I shall have.' Lord Hamilton shuttin menu book. 'The duck over the hills. And far away. And bring a bottle of champagne. Four glasses. Two straws.'

Oscar makin face. 'Daddy I grew out of drinking straws on my sixth birthday.'

'The straws are both for Tom.' Lord Hamilton sayin: 'The drinking straws are small here and Tom has rather a wide mouth.'

Me touch my mouth. It—

Me thinkin about dead boy.

Then.

Lord Hamilton sayin: 'Tom. Arent you hungry. You havent even touched your pudding. The rest of us are half way thru our main course.'

Me lookin at table. It is got plates on it a dinner. Every one eat a dinner a main course half way thru. Me got a puddin not eat it.

Me pick up spoon eat it a puddin.

Lord Hamilton got a knife a fork cut up that dinner a dead boy. Put it in mouth.

Oscar lookin round table. At every one at table. Do a cough a little one doin it pretend. Then. When every one look at that Oscar. Oscar sayin: 'Who stole all the apostrophes from market stalls and shop signs. Thats what I want to know.'

Every one doin laugh.

Lord Hamilton doin posh laugh sayin: 'Ho ho.'

Oscar sayin: 'Daddy Im brilliant arent I.'

'Yes darling I rather suppose you are.'

'Daddy. Daddy would you still love me if I was like Tom.'

Lord Hamilton lookin at me. I am eat a puddin. 'No. No I dont think so.'

Oscar smilin. He is brilliant aint he.

Every one eat a dinner.

Oscar sayin: 'Daddy can I have some of your snort.'

'Yes of course.'

Lady Eliza sayin: 'Oscar you know I dont approve of you taking your fathers cocaine.' Lady Eliza gettin out a tin out of pocket dress side front pocket sayin: 'Here use mine. Its cut with natural lipids to help soothe the delicate nostril lining.'

Me eatin puddin. It is pink it is on plate do a wobble. Me move that plate make it do wobble.

'Daddy.' Oscar puttin nose in tin sayin: 'Daddy you know when you were buggering me in the back passage. The maid saw us didnt she.'

'I dont know darling I wasnt wearing my contacts.' Lord Hamilton pickin up fone it is ringin not makin a noise. It is in visible he aint got it. Pick it up hold it at a ear sayin: 'Yes. Quite. Yes. Quite.' Puttin down fone turn it off. 'Tom Im afraid your parents still havent come forward.'

At other table. Big black man sat eat on a own. Puttin down fork lookin at me raisin a eye brow open a eye.

Lord Hamilton sayin: 'Tom where might they be. Might they have disowned you. Or abandoned you in some way.'

'Feed him to the lions Daddy.'

'Tom is there a telly fone number.' Lord Hamilton says: 'Your father. Or your mother.'

'Daddy try the inner city hot line.'

'No,' I say standin up. 'Dont feed me to a hot lion.'

'Tom why are you stood up.' Lord Hamilton sayin: 'If you need the toilet. Oscar take Tom to the toilet.'

Me sittin down.

At other table. Big black man sat eat on a own. Put down a fork. Stand up. Put on a jacket mauve posh one. Goin out of restaurant shuttin door.

Then.

Just when door is shuttin.

Door openin man comin in big black one same one. Jacket on in side out it aint that man it is a difrent one it is difrent. 'Excuse me.' Big black man sayin: 'Has any one seen a young boy named Tom. Im lookin for a young boy named Tom. His parents asked me to fetch him.'

129

Lord Hamilton lookin at big black man. At me. 'Well this is Tom.'

Big black man grinnin his white teeth. 'Tom. Are you Tom.'

Me noddin.

'Whats your last name Tom.'

'Boler,' I say sayin it.

'Boler.'

Me noddin.

Big black man noddin. 'Tom my name is Boxford. Your parents.' Boxford lookin at Lord Hamilton. 'Mister and Misses Boler. Asked me to fetch him. And look after him.'

Lord Hamilton standin up. 'Tom.'

Me standin up.

Lord Hamilton laughin. 'I was beginning to think we were stuck with him. Good bye Tom.'

Me goin out. Holdin a hand it is black.

Oscar sayin: 'Dont forget your moronic bear thing.'

Me goin out. Goin down street walkin. Holdin a hand it is black. It is black man hand a man he is young he is called Boxford he is doin a look after. He is hand some he is got a hand me holdin hand.

'So.' Boxford standin on street corner. 'Remind me Tom. Your parents disowned or abandoned you where. In the restaurant.'

Me shakin head.

'The theatre bar. One of the theatres.'

Me noddin. Then. Shakin head.

'Not in one of the theatres.'

Me shakin head.

'But you had been to the theatre. A night out. At the theatre.'

Me noddin.

'And your parents disowned or abandoned you in the theatre.'

Me shakin head.

Boxford takin off jacket mauve posh in side out turn it out side in. Put it on.

'That is what I went for,' I say.

'Because they disowned or abandoned you.'

Me noddin.

'So they disowned or abandoned you. So you went to the theatre.'

Me noddin.

Boxford walkin walkin me goin down road. 'But where actually were you. When they disowned or abandoned you.'

'My dad. Is in prison,' I say. 'My mum. Is havin a sex.'

Boxford noddin.

'Did they ask you to look after me.'

Boxford lookin a other way. Lookin in shop window a shop. 'They asked me to look after you. Until they are ready to take you back.'

'Are they goin a take me back then.'

Boxford walkin round corner take me round a corner. Standin at bus stop stoppin bus. Holdin out a hand it is black.

'Are my mum an dad goin a take me back then,' I say lookin at Boxford.

Boxford noddin.

Boxford gettin on bus gettin me on bus.

Me an Boxford on bus. It is London bus in London it is red. It smells it is got on it a man what smells. It is got a lady got kids tellin em off sayin: 'Shut up you little scraper.' It is got a groan up boy an girl dressed up like a ghost got on black clobes an make up it is white. It is got a man got a can of beer drink it that beer dribble down chin make it a beer beard it is funny makin me laugh. Me lookin at it laughin. Boxford lookin at it not laughin. Boxford lookin at me sayin: 'Nearly there.'

Me lookin at Boxford. He is doin a look after.

Me lookin out of window. It is London it is in the middle it is got big buildings they are posh. Then. It is got scruffy buildings they aint even big. Bus drivin stoppin at traffic lights it is dark got lights lightin it up red green an a yellow sort of one. Me lookin at yellow one sayin: 'What is that called.'

'That.' Boxford lookin at it. We are up stairs on bus lookin out front window sat at front. Boxford lookin out window at traffic lights sayin: 'Traffic lights.'

Me noddin.

'Whats with the bear.'

Me lookin at bear.

Boxford takin bear I am holdin it Boxford holdin it it is broke.

'It got broke,' I say. 'A boys. A boy got killed. I got it. I went out my house an ran a way.'

Boxford noddin.

'A boy got killed.'

Boxford lookin out of window.

Me an Boxford an Poll Tax Clown gettin off bus. Me holdin Poll Tax Clown in a arms not holdin a hand. Boxford walkin on pavement me walkin lookin be hind wavin at a bus it goin up road. Me an Boxford walkin on pavement goin up stairs it is a house it is old it is broke. Up stairs in a door it

132

aint even shut it is broke. Up in door stairs in house up a other stairs it is old it is got wall paper fallin off wall wall fallin off wall paper flowers fallin off.

Boxford goin up stairs sayin: 'Roxy.'

Roxy comin out of room. It is a lady a black lady got on make up got too much on. 'Did you get it.'

'Not exactly.'

'What do you mean not exactly.' Roxy comin out of room. Lookin down stairs at Boxford goin up stairs. Roxy lookin at me. Roxy sayin: 'O.'

Boxford noddin. Goin in room in door.

'Where did he come from.'

'I was having a nibble after the audition and—' Boxford sayin it shuttin door.

Me standin out side door.

Me sittin on stairs. At top of stairs.

Me holdin Poll Tax Clown. He is a bear he aint got a arms.

I have got four arms. Two of em Tom arms two of em bear arms in a trouser pocket of a trouser.

Door openin. Roxy comin out eatin a lip stick sayin: 'Hey.' Gettin down on a knees lookin at me smilin puttin round a arms. 'Im Roxy. Im your new mum.'

Me noddin.

Roxy lookin at me smilin.

'Are you my new mum.'

Roxy noddin.

Boxford comin out. Standin be hind new mum got a hand on a shoulder holdin shoulder. 'Just until your real mum and dad are ready to take you back.'

Me noddin. I have got a bear.

Roxy lookin at bear sayin: 'Whos this.'

'Poll Tax Clown.'

'Is that his name. Poll Tax Clown.'

Me noddin.

'Thats a funny name for a bear.' Roxy lookin up at Boxford. 'Thats a funny name for a bear isnt it Box.'

Boxford noddin.

'Hes a nice bear.' Roxy sayin: 'What happened to his eyes.'

'They got cut up,' I say sayin it.

'And his arms.'

'They got cut off,' I say sayin it. 'I have got it.' Me standin up. Got a arms in a trouser pocket what got bought a lady.

'I can fix him up for you. If you like.'

'Roxy makes costumes for the theatre. Some of them are very elaborate.'

Roxy standin up. 'Shall I get him fixed up.'

Me an black lady Roxy an big black man Boxford goin in door in room. It is a bed room it is big. In it is a lot of costumes hung up. Under it is a bed carnt see it got on it costumes.

Roxy holdin up costume. 'This isnt quite finished yet.' Roxy lookin down at costume. It is a dress got flowers on it fallin off.

Me holdin my bear. I have got it.

'Roxy sort out his bear.'

Roxy got a sew it machine. It is hidin under a dresses. Roxy gettin dresses offof it throwin on floor they aint finish. Under it is sew it machine. It is shape like a arm got a needle do sew. Turn on that machine it is sew it machine same as in the shops.

Boxford sayin: 'Roxys going to mend your bear. Your Poll Tax Clown.'

Me lookin at Poll Tax Clown.

134

Roxy puttin hands black on lap. Pattin on lap.

Me puttin Poll Tax Clown on lap.

'Have you got the arms.'

Me take em out of trouser pocket they have got stuff comin out give em to Roxy.

Roxy gettin a thing. It is a needle funny shape it is for pickin. Roxy puttin it round shape of bear shape open it out. Pickin it off that sew un do it. Cotton sew comin off. Bear get open up. Roxy puttin pick thing round that head an that shoulder arm hole holder an round that bear tum an bear leg an a other arm hole holder an round that head at top of head.

Boxford pattin on a side of bed.

Me sittin on bed. Be side Boxford.

Roxy openin up out bear gettin out stuff in out. It is white it is bear blood put it on that costumes it aint finish. Roxy got that bear half it is front half got a face makin it a bear. Put a finger thru eye hole wiggle it. It is cross shape cut in a eye. Roxy got a needle an a fred. Roxy puttin needle in fred fred it thru needle eye hole wriggle it. Roxy sewin up that cross cut in a eye.

Me an Boxford watchin.

Then.

In a other room.

Telly fone ringin. Boxford hearin it lookin at Roxy sayin: 'Shall I get it.'

'If you dont mind. Im mending bears. Tell them Im mending bears.'

'It could be my father. I asked him to ring me about the you know what.' Boxford goin out of bed room. Goin up down stairs. Get a fone pick it up. 'Hello Roxys residence. O hello Dad. Yes well you would find me here thats because Im here. I practically live here. Practically.'

Roxy laughin.

Me sittin on bed side. Boxford is in a other room on a fone doin talk. It comin up down stairs. Comin in room. Boxford talkin on fone sayin: 'Dad you know what I want to do.'

Roxy doin sew.

'Dad of course I want to go to theatre school. I want to follow in your foot steps.'

Roxy laughin. Doin sew.

'Dad if you know it. Then why ask me.'

Roxy sewin up cross cut in a eye.

'I just dont want to end up in some crappy little fringe thing. This is why. It is so important. That I attend theatre school.'

Roxy noddin.

'But Dad I have nothing. One can not build on nothing. I need an education.' Boxford not sayin nothin. Then. Sayin: 'And I need you to pay for it.'

Roxy lookin at me. Makin a face. It is got too much make up on it.

Boxford puttin down telly fone. Walk up an down a stairs makin a noise doin it cross got shoes on. Open a door. Shut it slam it a door not even goin out it. Comin in room. Sittin down on bed next to be side me. Put black hands in lap. Lookin at hands. Lookin up. Lookin at Roxy sayin: 'That was my father on the bone.'

'And.'

'And he wont cough up.' Boxford foldin a arms. 'Bastard can afford it.'

'He wants you to make your own way in the world Box. What about the other thing. The loan.'

Boxford shakin head. 'He said we should get an over giraffe. We already have an over fucking giraffe.'

'Then youll just have to get a job then wont you Box. My costume making carnt support us both.'

Boxford noddin. Not smilin.

Roxy foldin up bear un fold it. Cut fred with a teeth got lip stick on it. Holdin up bear un fold it. It un foldin with the holdin.

'My father owns three houses. Fuck knows how. Spends half his life on the toilet.'

Roxy laughin.

'No one needs three houses Roxy. I know hes fat but. He could put one buttock in each house and still have one to spare. One house I mean not one buttock.'

Roxy gettin a button box. Gettin out a buttons. Holdin em up show em. 'These for eyes.'

Me noddin.

'You need to get a job Boxford.' Roxy sewin a eye a button a bear. Roxy lookin at Boxford. Bear eye lookin at Boxford.

'I am not sacrificing my acting career to help pay your bloody mort gage. We have to think of something else. Well we have thought of something else.' Boxford standin up.

'Youre going to fone Robert Tablet.'

Boxford sitting down. 'No. We try this new thing first.'

Me holdin bear it is mended. Roxy sewin on it a eyes it is buttons. Roxy sewed it round a edge. Round head an that shoulder arm hole holder an round that bear tum an bear leg an a other arm hole holder an round that head at top of head. Sewin it on a arms on a bear. Holdin it up smilin sayin: 'There. There there there. All better.'

Me holdin bear.

Roxy goin up stairs half up it is a door it is half way up a stairs. Roxy openin it sayin: 'This is your room in here.'

Me goin in room it is little. It is got in it a bed it is little. On it is a costumes carnt see it.

'Lets shift some of this stuff.' Roxy gettin a costumes throw it down stairs it landin on Boxford on head.

Boxford big an black got costumes on sayin: 'Roxy Im on the fone.'

Roxy laughin.

Boxford gettin off that costumes sayin: 'David about your special request.'

Roxy throwin costumes down stairs.

Costumes landin on Boxford. 'Roxy Im in a bad enough mood as it is.'

Roxy laughin.

Me lookin at costumes. Laughin.

'David youre a fickle one David.' Boxford gettin off costumes holdin fone sayin: 'Eight hundred euros David. Cash.'

Roxy gettin a sheet it is white. Roxy throwin sheet down stairs it landin on Boxford makin it like a ghost. Boxford a ghost talk on fone gettin cross.

Me in bed. Roxy readin it a bed time story. It is a story it is called: The Princess and the Plastic. Roxy readin it sayin: 'And then they went to the shops. And then. They went to the car park and put the groceries in the car. And then they got in to the car. And then they went home. And then they put the groceries in the fridge.'

Me in bed. Got a bear a Poll Tax Clown snugged up. Got knees up got blanky round it it is cold in room it is spring but it aint spring in Roxy house it is old it is cold.

Roxy readin story sayin: 'And then. They went to the woods. And then they had a picnic. And then they played with the ball. And then the ball rolled down the hill. And then. They ran down the hill and kicked the ball up the hill. And then. They put the ball in the car.'

Me lookin round room. It is little got ceiling wonky like it is fallin down but it aint it is wonky.

'And then.' Roxy readin story. 'They sat on the blanket. And then. And then. They went home. And then.'

Me lookin at Roxy. She is nice a nice lady a new mum. She is young but groan up got make up on. She is black got hair funny made of mud same as on the telly on Terry Telly at home I watched it.

Roxy sayin: 'And then.' Roxy sayin: 'And then.' Roxy sayin: 'The end.' Roxy shuttin book.

'Read it again.'

Boxford comin in room lookin at Roxy doin a thumbs up. Boxford sittin on side of bed be side Roxy. Boxford sayin: 'Tom. This room.'

Me lookin at Boxford.

Roxy sayin: 'We hope youre going to be happy here Tom.'

Me noddin.

Roxy smilin. Put black hands on cheek of Tom. Tom put hand on cheek of Poll Tax Clown a bear.

Boxford sayin: 'This room. Its really nothing to worry about Tom. We have to tell you something about this room.'

Me noddin.

'This room.' Boxford says: 'Is haunted.'

Me not noddin. Hair standin on a end. Roxy puttin hand on hair head brush Tom hair with a hand make it lay down go a sleep.

'Its nothing to worry about Tom. Its a friendly ghost.' Boxford laughin sayin: 'Actually perhaps a little too friendly.'

Roxy pokin Boxford in a elbow arm.

'Yes any way. Its nothing to worry about.' Boxford sayin it is nothin to worry about sayin: 'Its not just one ghost actually you may get visited by a different ghost each night. Haunted I mean not visited haunted. You may get haunted by a different ghost each night.'

Poll Tax Clowns hair fur stand on a end.

'I always find Tom. Its best to lay on your front. With your head. Under the pillow like so.' Boxford pickin up pillow put it on head a hat.

Roxy laughin.

Repetitive Brain Injury

Boxford an Roxy are havin a party. Roxy makin a jelly makin it wobble put it in fridge. Boxford cut out a paper cave men cut em out of paper joined up hang em up. Boxford puttin chair in kitchen stand on it put a arms in a air. Me handin him em paper cave men. Boxford puttin em up poke em a drawing pin. Boxford gettin off chair paper cave men hangin on kitchen ceiling touchin carpet. Me helpin movin chair put it at a other side of kitchen. Boxford pickin up that paper cave men other end. Boxford stand on chair put a arms in a air. Puttin em up paper cave men poke em a drawing pin. Boxford gettin off chair lookin up at paper cave men. 'There.'

Roxy puttin jelly in fridge. 'There.'

Me sayin: 'What jelly is it.'

'What flavour.' Roxy says: 'Orange squash flavour. Do you like orange squash flavour.'

Me noddin. I do like it.

Roxy goin out of room.

Me openin fridge. Lookin at jelly.

Roxy an Boxford are my new mum. I am lived here for two weeks an two days an one month. It is near my school it is. One hour fifteen minutes walk. I saw it we went to a shops.

Roxy comin in me shuttin fridge. 'Nice paper cave men Box. Tom do you want to blow up some balloons.'

Me shakin head.

Roxy got balloons. They are dead not blowed up. Roxy openin packet bitin it gettin out a balloons.

Roxy givin me one of balloons it is blue.

Roxy puttin a balloon end in a mouth blowin it up a huff an a poof.

Me put balloon end in mouth.

Roxy sayin: 'Blow.'

Me doin it but. Carnt do it.

Roxy sayin: 'Blow.'

Me doin it but. Carnt do it.

Roxy takin balloon pull it make it stretch hold it in a hand. Balloon stretchin gettin long. Roxy givin me it.

Me put balloon end in mouth. Blow it it goin up a bit makin squeak noise goin fallin on floor.

Roxy laughin.

Door knock knockin on door.

Boxford shoutin down stairs shoutin: 'Come in the doors open.'

Sound of front door openin some one comin in.

Boxford goin to top of stairs lookin down stairs. Me an Boxford lookin down stairs. It is the beer man got beer. Boxford sayin: 'Its the beer man.'

Beer man shoutin up stairs: 'Thatll be twenty five euros fifty.' Beer man got a beer belly holdin on it a beer box of beer. Puttin beer box on carpet stair. Goin out door. Come back in got a other beer belly box. Put it on carpet stair.

Boxford goin in kitchen. 'Roxy have we got some money for the beer man.'

'Take it from the you know what money.'

Boxford open a drawer get out it a envelope. It is got in it money. I have seen it. It has got wrote on it: ghost money.

Me an Boxford goin down stairs. Boxford sayin: 'Is that the lot.'

Beer man puttin down boxes. Gettin a boxes. Puttin down boxes sayin: 'Right thats the lot.'

Boxford countin money. Countin it in to hand of beer man sayin: 'Fifteen twenty twenty five. Here take thirty. Buy your self a new frock.'

Beer man doin face. Beer man goin out door. Shuttin door.

Boxford open box card board box. It is got in it beer cans of beer. 'Tom do you want to help carry these up.'

Me an Boxford carryin up stairs. Carpet gettin broke flowers fallin offof it. Boxford carryin a box it is big Boxford is big got a box. Me carryin a box but. Carnt do it I am little. Me carryin a beer can of beer. Get it out of box carryin it up stairs.

Boxford puttin card board beer box on kitchen table.

Me put can of beer on kitchen table.

Roxy laughin.

Boxford lookin at can of beer shakin head. 'Tom why dont you help Roxy.'

'Tom do you want to help me stick the dicks.'

Me doin face.

'Dicks.' Roxy holdin up a sausage. 'Sausages.' Roxy lookin at me laughin holdin up a sausage on a stick. 'Dicks on sticks. For the party.'

Me an Roxy makin a dicks on a sticks. Roxy gettin sausages a tray metal out of ye olde micro wavy overn. Put it on table. It is got on it sausages. Roxy got a box little got in it sticks. Me an Roxy get a sticks stick it in a dick.

Door knock knockin on door.

Boxford shoutin down stairs shoutin: 'Come in the doors broken.'

Sound of front door openin some one comin in.

Me sayin: 'Its the beer man.'

Boxford shakin head.

Boxford goin to top of stairs lookin down stairs. Boxford sayin: 'Its the wine man.'

Me goin to top of stairs. Holdin dick on stick.

Wine man sayin: 'That will be. Lets have a look.' Wine man havin a look at a clip board. 'Thirty six euros sixty.' Wine man got a mouse mos tosh it is posh. Wine man got a box put it on carpet stair. Goin out door. Come back in got a other box it is posh. Put it on carpet stair.

Boxford goin in kitchen. 'Shall I take it out of the erm—'

Roxy noddin.

Roxy gettin sausage stick pricks off table. Funny hair man puttin decks on table. Settin up a decks.

Me open fridge look at jelly.

Funny hair man settin up decks plug it in. Funny hair man got a wires plug it in a back of decks. Got a head fone plug it in. Put it on head.

Boxford thinkin. Sayin: 'Something you can dance to. But. Faster. So you have to take lots of drugs.'

Funny hair man laughin. 'Ive got tons of this sort of stuff.'
Funny hair man got a record put it on decks. Put a needle
on it a record. Music comin out it is loud. It is fast. It is
music. It is a same a noise.

Boxford noddin. Laughin.

Me put finger in jelly in fridge do a lick.

Roxy got head in cubberd carnt see it. Roxy sayin:
'Something we can dance to.'

'There isnt room to dance Roxy.'

Funny hair man sayin: 'Aint you got another room.'

'Theres the bath room.' Boxford says: 'And Toms room.
Which is the size of a match box. People are basically going
to have to dance on the stairs.'

'What about our room. We could put the bed in the
garden.'

'Do we have a garden.' Boxford lookin out window. 'I
didnt know we had a garden.'

'Yes well youre an introvert.'

Boxford laughin.

Me lookin at Roxy. At Boxford.

Then.

Lift my tee shirt Boxford bought it got on it a face. Lift
it up. Put in it jelly bowl of jelly. Pull down tee shirt got on
it a face. Jelly touchin tum. Jelly bowl hid under tee shirt
touchin tum.

Shut fridge door run up half stairs in bed room.

Me layin on bed. Lift up tee shirt face got jelly bowl pressin
on tum up side down. Turnin get bowl offof it jelly ploppin
out of bowl stuck on tum.

Me laughin got jelly on tum. It doin wobble on tum. It
is cold it is doin wobble. Me movin tum make it do wobble.

Me turnin tip jelly in bowl.

Jelly in bowl it is broke. Put finger in it lick it I like it. It is squash orange it is nice I like it.

Look at my tum. It is got jelly bits on it stuck on it. Me wipe it off tum wipe it on a Poll Tax Clown. He is got ghost on it white wiped on it. Ghost wipin it on it. On Poll Tax Clown on bear tum. Me wipe jelly wobble on it on Poll Tax Clown on bear bare tum.

It is a party it is Roxy an Boxfords party. It is noisy got that music a same a noise. It is night it is got lights off special ones on flash on an off.

Me goin down half way stairs. Got tum ache.

It is a lot of people in party touchin tums an bums carnt get past. Me gettin past goin under a legs. Me goin in kitchen. Black lady Roxy wearin black dress a party dress. Got make up on it got too much on. Holdin on shoulder of Tom sayin: 'Gotcha.'

'I didnt eat it.'

'Tom it was your jelly. Tom come and meet Robert. Tom this is Robert Tablet.' Roxy talkin to big red hair man got big pockets. 'Robert this is Tom.'

Robert Tablet lookin down at Tom laughin pattin on head.

'Robert give Tom one of your spangles.'

Robert Tablet shakin head. 'Hes not old enough. Hes not tall enough.' Robert Tablet holdin out hand.

Roxy says: 'Tom. Jump.'

Me doin a jump.

Big red hair man Robert Tablet sayin: 'You have to be as tall as Robs hand. To take a ride on the magic spangle trip.'

Roxy laughin.

Me doin jump. Head touchin hand.

Roxy sayin: 'Did he make the grade.'

'They grow up fast.' Robert Tablet gettin out a sweety gettin it out of pocket out of bag. Gettin bag out of pocket. It is little see thru full up of sweets. Gettin out a sweet givin it.

Me put it in mouth.

'Tom you have to swallow it with water. Its not a sweety.' Roxy gettin a water. Askin a lady get it. Lady turnin turnin on tap put water in glass of water. Turnin off tap. Turnin passin it to Roxy. Roxy give me it. Roxy sayin: 'It wont do anything for an hour.'

Robert Tablet noddin. 'It takes about an hour.'

Me take water drink it swallow sweet. It is touched my tongue it is yuck.

Roxy turnin round talkin to a man a lady.

Robert Tablet talkin to a lady a man.

Me goin under legs. Goin down stairs be tween every one what is standin on stairs doin dancin.

There is a lady posh one got on big posh hat. Me goin up to lady sayin: 'Are you Prim.'

Lady lookin down at Tom.

'You are like Prim. She is my new mum. Prim is. My old one. My old new mum.'

Posh lady laughin. Drinkin a wine.

'Am I the smallest Tom in the party.'

Posh lady carnt hear it is a noise a music. Gettin bendin down. Put a ear to a small Tom.

'Am I the smallest Tom in the party.'

Posh lady lookin at party. Posh lady lookin at me at Tom. Posh lady laughin noddin.

'I have got ghosts in my bum.'

Posh lady laughin. 'A haunted bum. How daft.'

Me noddin.

Then.

Music stoppin.

Boxford comin in Roxy comin in. Robert Tablet comin in. Boxford sayin: Every one. Roxy sayin: Every one.

Every one shuttin up.

Roxy sayin: 'Come out to the road. Every one come out to the road. We have an announcement. To make.'

Every one lookin at every one.

Every one goin down stairs. Lookin at every one.

Out in road. Every one standin in road. Party comin out of house flat. Down in door stairs. Down out door steps. Out in road.

When every one out it. Roxy an Boxford standin at top of steps. Stand in light of door of where they live.

Boxford holdin out hands makin every one do quiet.

Every one sayin: Shh. Shh.

Boxford sayin: 'Right. An announcement. Firstly. We would like to thank you all for coming. To our coming out party.'

Every one laughin.

'And when I say coming out party. That isnt why weve come out here.' Boxford holdin out hand at the night it is got stars in it. 'Weve come out here because there isnt room in side for the announcement.'

Roxy sayin: 'Its a big announcement.'

Every one laughin.

Boxford says: 'Theres another reason why its a coming out party. Isnt there Roxy.'

Roxy noddin. Laughin.

'But before we get to that.' Boxford clearin throat. 'Those of you who have known me for a long time. Will know that. For a long time. I have wanted to go to theatre school. And become an actor. Rather than just a liar.'

Every one laughin.

'I have now raised funding and start at the Piccalilli School in the autumn.'

Every one doin clap hands. Some one sayin: Hooray.

Me standin at front of every one in road at kerb edge. Standin on kerb gettin big.

Boxford sayin: 'Now. The coming out.'

Some one laughin.

Boxford clearin throat.

No one sayin nothin.

'Now. Those of you who know me. Will know. My girl friend here Roxy.' Boxford holdin out hand at Roxy.

Roxy smilin.

'But what you may not know. Is. That Roxy—'

Roxy takin off dress. It is party dress at party. Roxy takin it off it is black. Roxy is black a lady takin off dress droppin it on out door steps.

'—is actually—'

Roxy standin got on under wear knickers an bra. Roxy takin off bra takin out socks droppin it on steps. Roxy takin off knickers. Standin. Holdin out a arms. Got no clobes on. Got a willy.

'—a man.'

No one sayin nothin.

'Wait theres more.' Boxford takin off shirt. Un button it take it off. Take off a shoe an a socks. Take it off drop it on steps. Take off trouser. 'Not only am I gay. But. I am also—' Boxford gettin Roxy dress hold it up. Put it on. Pull it over head put it on a dress. 'A transvestite. Now. Any questions.'

No one sayin nothin.

Me pointin at willy of Roxy.

*

It is a music a noise a same. Every one doin dancin. Every one jump up an down it is fast doin it fast. Every one touchin a back of Tom. Tom fallin over groan up hand on back make me not fall over. Every one hold out a hand make me not fall over. It is a best hand. It is a best party.

That man. Me pointin at man. He is a best man. Me goin up to man sayin: 'Youre the best man.'

Man not sayin nothin.

Me holdin on leg of man do leg hug.

Man lookin down.

'Youre the best man.'

He carnt hear it it is a music a noise a same.

It is a best music what ever I ever heard it is. A best one. Me jumpin up an down doin best dance what ever I ever did done. Then. Doin a other one the same one.

Me goin under legs of a man a lady a other man. Goin under a lot of em make em fall over. Every one spill it a drink landin on a head of Tom.

Me crawlin under a legs goin in that lot of people. Under a legs of a man a lady a other man. Goin under em make em fall over. Come out in a lot of people standin up jump about muck about. Every one laughin. Every one touchin a head of Tom. It is a best—

Every one has got a funny face. I have got it it is on my tee shirt.

Me lookin at people what are at party. Hold on a legs of man sayin: 'Lift me up.'

Man liftin me up.

Me lookin at face of people at party. It is a lot of people got a lot of difrent face. It is funny a clown. Every one is a clown. Me laughin pointin at clown.

Man puttin me down.

Where is a kitchen. Where is Roxy an Boxford got on a dress. Me lookin for Roxy an Boxford. People gettin out a way in the way. Some one spill a beer a drink. Me open my mouth catch it drink it. Pullin on leg of man sayin: 'Can I drink it.'

Man lookin down at Tom. It is a clown a funny man.

Me pointin at funny face of man sayin: 'Youre a clown.'

'Why am I a clown.'

'Every one is,' I say. 'It is a party of clown house.'

Man not laughin.

Me laughin. 'Where is a kitchen where is Roxy.' Me gettin in kitchen. It is got a lot of clowns in it. Me touchin clowns sayin: 'Clowns. Youre a clowns you are.'

Clown lady touchin on a arm sayin: 'Tom are you alright. Are you enjoying your pill.'

Clown man sayin: 'Did you give him a spangle.'

'Robert gave him one.'

Me sayin at clown man: 'Youre a clown you are.'

Clown lady laughin.

Clown man not laughin. 'Youre just fucked on your pill.' Clown man lookin at clown lady sayin: 'Dont give him any more.'

'Robert gave him it.'

'Well dont let Robert give him any more. We do have to pay for them you know.'

'Its a party Box.' Clown lady sayin: 'Get out of your box.'

'I think I will. Every one else is. Wheres Robert.'

Me sayin: 'Wheres Roxy.'

'Im Roxy. Im going to find Robert.' Clown lady goin out of kitchen.

Me followin clown lady. Gettin lost come out of kitchen goin in kitchen lookin for Roxy but—

O. It is got clowns in it. O I like clowns. They are funny. Me pointin at funny clowns.

Clowns sayin: 'Blah blah blah.'

Me holdin on a clown sayin: 'Lift me up.'

Man clown liftin me up holdin me up. 'What do you want to look at. Do you want to look out of the window.' Man holdin me at window.

Me lookin out of window. 'O. Its snowin.'

Every one lookin at window.

Clown man lookin at window. 'Its spring.'

'Snow,' I say glass touchin on nose.

'Wheres snow.'

Me pointin.

'Theyre stars.'

'What they fallin down for then.'

Man shakin head.

'Look,' I say pointin. 'A snow man.'

'Thats a rubbish bin.'

'Can I play in it.'

'What. In a rubbish bin.' Clown man puttin me down.

'Its snowin,' I say lookin at clowns. 'O. You are a clowns.'

Fat clown lady bendin on knee got a wine sayin: 'Are you alright.'

'Look,' I say pointin at clowns. 'Clowns.'

'I like clowns Tom. Would you like some wine.' Fat clown lady givin me a wine.

Me holdin wine. It is in a cup paper plastic a party. It is red it is a clown nose drink. Me drinkin clown nose drink it is red.

On kitchen table. Next to a decks. Next to a records. It is a drink of it. Some one put it on it. Me pick it up pourin it in my one drink it. A clown nose drink it is red.

Other lady tall one look at me sayin: 'Are you drinking wine.'

'It is clown nose drink.'

'Do you want one of these.' Tall lady holdin out it in a hand. It is got sweets in it. 'Theyre really fun.'

Me take it eat it.

'Not too many.'

Me countin it. One two three. Put em in mouth drink it a clown nose drink.

Tall lady laughin.

'Is it a sweets.'

'Dont do any more will you. Theyre really fun.'

'Is it a clown sweets,' I say lookin at clown nose drink clown sweets.

'Why do you keep on about clowns. Do you like clowns. Are you going to join the circus. When you grow up.'

'Every one is a clown.'

Tall lady goin a way a clown.

It is a clown party but. There aint a clowns.

Me goin up to a man. Holdin on a trouser sayin: 'Where is a clowns.'

Man sayin: 'Bring on the clowns.'

Me laughin.

Man liftin me up holdin me up in a air. 'Bring on the clowns.' Movin doin a dance.

Me laughin.

Man puttin me down.

'Lift me up.'

Man liftin me up. 'How old are you.'

'Nine.'

'And youre at a party. Shouldnt you be in bed.'

'There is people in it.' I went up an went in a bed room. It is got people in it. A man jumpin a bout on a lady doin dance got no clobes on.

Man puttin me down.

'Lift me up.'

Man liftin me up. Put a Tom on a shoulder sayin: 'We are the champions.'

Me puttin arms in a air.

'Hold on to me. Thats it.'

Me holdin on man on hair head.

'You can do it with one hand.' Man puttin hand in a air sayin: 'We are the champions.'

Me puttin one hand in a air sayin it sayin: 'I am a champions.'

Man walkin me round party sayin it.

'Tom.' Roxy sayin it sayin: 'I hear that youre the champion. Is that right.'

'Yeah I am. I am tall.' Me holdin hand on top of head of Roxy hair mud.

Boxford smilin sayin: 'Are you fucked Tom.'

'Spangled. And hes only ten.'

'Nine,' I say. I am nine.

'Roxy was rounding up wasnt you Roxy. To the nearest multiple of ten.'

'That makes me forty. And you thirty. I feel old Box.'

'Lets do some more pills.' Boxford sayin: 'Wheres Robert Tablet.'

Man puttin me down. A champion.

Roxy lookin over there. 'Over there I think. By the sink.'

'Look. Father Christmas.'

Roxy laughin. 'Thats not Father Christmas Tom thats Robert.'

'He is got a red hat on.'

'Thats his hair. Hes got long red hair. Hes a hippy. Sort of.'

'He is got,' I say. 'A white Father Christmas beard.'

'Thats his beer.' Roxy sayin to Father Christmas: 'Its got a bit of a head on it. Have you got a big enough head on that beer Rob.'

Father Christmas pourin can of beer in a beard. Lookin at beard it is white. 'Some ones been shaking them up.' Holdin beer can sayin: 'Theyre all like it.'

Me pattin red tum of Father Christmas. 'Are you Father Christmas.'

Father Christmas laughin.

Roxy sayin: 'You do have the stomach for it.'

Father Christmas gettin out a bag out of a pocket.

'Yeah it is Father Christmas. He is got presents.'

Father Christmas put hand in sack. Gettin out it a presents a sweets.

Roxy sayin: 'Well we have been good all year.' Holdin out hand.

Father Christmas puttin in it a presents.

Boxford holdin out hand.

Father Christmas puttin in it a presents.

Me holdin out hand.

Father Christmas put—

O.

'We need to make a profit.' Boxford sayin: 'That reminds me Paul Pot wanted twelve but I carnt locate the greasy bugger.'

'I know where he is,' I say.

'Well take these to him.'

Father Christmas puttin presents in a hand of Boxford.

Boxford countin em puttin em in hand of Tom. 'Tom dont fuck this up. Dont eat them. If you eat them. You pay for them. Out of your pocket money. Roxy does Tom get pocket money.'

'We should sort that out. You gave him the tee shirt.'

Me lookin down at tee shirt. Got on it a face.

Where is that Paul Pot. Me goin up to every one sayin it sayin: 'Where is that Paul Pot.'

Every one dancin. Not sayin.

Me eatin sweets. Drinkin it a clown nose drink it is red. Goin up to man sayin: 'Where is that Paul that Pot.'

'He went up stairs.'

Other man sayin: 'Hes shaggin his bird up stairs.'

Me goin up stairs. It is a stairs made of clowns. Me treddin on clowns. Clown nose makin a beep beep it is clowns it is funny makin me laugh. Open a door made of clowns. Lookin in it.

There is a people in it. A lady a man. When I went in it. Man jumpin a bout on lady got no clobes on. It is the same man the same lady. Man an lady puttin clobes on. Man sayin: 'Its alright you can come in.'

Me goin in. It is my room. It is got Poll Tax Clown in it. Me lookin round room sayin: 'Where is my Poll Tax Clown.'

'Your what.'

'My bear got funny name.'

'O him.' Man gettin out of bed got no socks on gettin bear out of be hind window curtain. Man gettin back in bed. 'We didnt want to corrupt him.'

'Thats right. We were doing things. Groan up things. And we didnt want him to see.'

Me lookin at lady. Lookin close at lady at face of lady. Sayin: 'Miss Kind.'

Lady holdin hand over face.

Man openin mouth. 'No. Dont tell me hes one of yours Helen.'

'Shh.' Miss Kind hittin man on a under covers arm.

'She aint Helen,' I say pointin at lady Miss Kind. 'She is Miss Kind.'

Man laughin.

Miss Kind hidin face.

'She is at school. A teacher. Doin teach.'

Man laughin.

'She is nice she is. You dont even get told off. Only Andrew Hand. He is naughty he is. Andrew Hand is.'

Man laughin.

Miss Kind not laughin. Holdin on man under covers. 'Tom I think youre confusing me with some one else.'

Man pattin on side of bed gettin me sat on side of bed. 'Tom this is my girl friend Helen. She does look like Miss Kind doesnt she. She actually won a Miss Kind look a like contest. Didnt you Helen.'

Miss Kind laughin.

'Shes nice she is. Miss Kind is.'

Man laughin. Sittin up on a knees.

'I didnt go a school for ages. Then. When I went a school. I didnt even get told off.' Man sittin on side of bed my one got a Miss Kind in it. 'That lady Prim what was doin look after. I am waited out side. Prim told Miss Kind I am scared of get told off. Then. When I went in it. I didnt even get told off.'

Man laughin.

'Tom.' Miss Kind sayin it kind sayin: 'Or what ever your name is. I think I heard some one call you Tom. Thats how I know your name is Tom. Now Tom. Im being completely honest with you Tom. Arent I Paul.'

Me lookin at man sayin: 'Are you Paul Pot.'

Man doin nod. He is Paul Pot.

'O,' I say puttin hand in trouser pocket. 'I have got a present for you. From Father Christmas. From Boxford.'

'The pills.'

Me got hand in pocket. Then. Sayin: 'O.'

'O what.'

Me got hand in pocket. 'I did a eat.'

'You ate them.'

Me noddin.

'You ate my pills.'

'It is a sweets,' I say on bed. 'I am a little boy.'

'Shit Paul how many were there.'

'Tom.' Paul Pot sayin: 'How many. Did they give you. Did Boxy give you.'

'It is more than ten,' I say holdin up a hand a fingers. 'It is. Twelve.'

Paul Pot lookin at Miss Kind. He is got a long hair at the back. 'Yeah twelve six each.'

'We should take him to hospital.'

'No Helen these arent proper pills these are more like a head fuck.' Paul Pot gettin out a cigs out of trouser pocket. 'You better stay with us. How long ago did you take them.'

Me pointin at door. 'It is out there. It is ten minutes ago. Or.' Me shruggin.

Miss Kind pattin on bed next to be side. 'Climb in here.'

Me gettin in bed proper. Under a covers. In be tween Miss Kind.

Paul Pot got out a cigs out of pocket sayin: 'Shall I skin up. Dont watch Tom. More groan up stuff.'

No one sayin nothin.

Miss Kind shakin head.

Miss Kind puttin hand on face.

Miss Kind puttin arms round a Tom.

No one sayin nothin.

Paul Pot makin a cigarette. Gettin out a cigarette. Lick it. Open it out. Get out a cig brown stuff. Put it in a bit of paper. Put in it a green stuff a leafs. Roll it up. Lick it. Flick it. Stick it. Paul Pot got out a lighter flame light it.

No one sayin nothin.

Then. Me sayin: 'Can we do magic carpet.'

'You actually did that.' Paul Pot smilin. 'That was my idea.'

Miss Kind smilin. Noddin.

'You are Miss Kind aint you.'

'I told you. Im Helen.'

Paul Pot lookin at me sayin: 'Have you really taken twelve pills.'

'An a other ones. A lady give me. A clown.'

'How many other ones.'

'One two three.' Me countin on a fingers. 'Three. O an Robert Tablet gaved me one.'

'Sixteen spangles.' Paul Pot smokin cig it is big. 'Shit.'

'Can we do magic carpet.'

Miss Kind shakin head. 'You ran off last time.'

'It is a magic run. I am do it now watch.'

Me standin up.

Me gettin off bed fallin off bed.

Me shoutin fallin off bed. Fallin down a hole.

Miss Kind an Paul Pot pull me out of hole sayin: 'Tom.'

Paul Pot sayin: 'Stay on the bed.'

Miss Kind sayin: 'Stay on the bed Tom. Hold on to me.'

Me holdin on Miss Kind but. I aint got a arms.

'Tom.'

'I aint got a arms,' I say sayin it to Miss Kind.

Miss Kind holdin arm holders shoulders sayin: 'You have got arms. Look these are your arms. Look. Whats this.'

'A hole,' I say lookin at hole.

'Its an arm. A lovely Tom arm. Isnt it Paul.'

Paul Pot lookin at hole. 'Its definitely an arm.'

'A big strong arm.' Miss Kind sayin it kind sayin: 'My big strong boy.'

'Miss Kind are you goin a way.'

'No Tom Im staying here with you. In your nice room.'

Me lookin at room. Pointin. 'There was a door there but. There aint a door.'

Miss Kind lookin at Paul Pot.

Paul Pot lookin at Miss Kind. Lookin at me. 'Tom. What can you see. Tell us what you can see.'

'There is.' Me pointin. 'There is a wall there aint a door.'

Paul Pot gettin off bed. 'There is a door watch.' Paul Pot gettin off bed goin in hole got eat up. 'See.' Paul Pot come out of hole. Gettin on bed. Next to be side a Tom.

Me holdin on Paul Pot. 'Dont get off bed. It is a hole.'

'Tom there is no hole.'

'It might be better to go with it.' Miss Kind sayin: 'Tom tell us where the hole is. We dont want to fall down a hole do we Paul.'

Paul noddin.

Me pointin at hole but. There aint even a hole.

Me gettin off bed. Standin on floor of carpet. It is old it is got flowers on it comin off. Carpet gettin broke makin a string. Me standin on carpet turnin lookin round at Paul Pot an Miss Kind. Paul Pot an Miss Kind holdin hands. Paul Pot an Miss Kind sat in bed of Tom got covers on. Me standin look at Miss Kind sayin: 'Is it a party.'

'It is a party Tom yes. Your party. You and Roxy and

Boxford. Listen.' Miss Kind doin all ears sayin: 'You can hear the music.'

Me listenin.

'Can you hear the music.'

Me shakin head.

'You carnt hear the music.'

Paul Pot smokin cig sayin: 'Doom doom doom doom.' Paul Pot movin head doin shape of music. Shakin it in head. Long hair movin at back of head.

Miss Kind sayin: 'Do you want to dance Tom.'

Me shakin head.

'You dont want to dance. Thats fine we dont have to dance.'

'Is it a party,' I say pointin at door.

Miss Kind sayin: 'Its a door. If you open the door. You can see the party.'

'Are you goin a way.'

Miss Kind shakin head.

Miss Kind an Paul Pot holdin hands.

Door openin Tom holdin it open it. It is a party but. There aint a party.

'Can you see the people.' Miss Kind sayin it kind sayin: 'I can see them from here. Carnt you Paul.'

Paul Pot sayin: 'Theres a woman dancing on the stairs. Wearing a boob tube. No thats a man. A man and a woman. The man wearing a boob tube. A wig. Smoking a cigar. Down the stairs theres people dancing I can see their heads. Its a party Tom everyones really happy having a good time.'

'Tom.' Miss Kind says: 'Carnt you see the people.'

Me shakin head.

'What can you see Tom.'

Me lookin out of door. 'There aint a out side.'

'Out side what.'

'Out side of room.' Me turnin. Lookin in room. Lookin at bed. There aint a bed.

'Tom.' Some one sayin it but. No one sayin it.

'What is that sayin it,' I say sayin it.

No one sayin.

No one sayin nothin.

Not even sayin.

Me holdin door handle. Look at hand holdin it. It is a Tom hand it is little. It is holdin a door handle. It is a cuddle a door hand handle cuddle. It is a only cuddle what I got. There aint a Miss Kind. There aint a Roxy. There aint a my mum there aint a cuddle.

Me sayin: 'Where is a cuddle.'

Miss Kind not sayin nothin. There aint a Miss Kind.

Miss Kind holdin on Tom sayin: 'Heres a cuddle. Let go of the door. Come over to the bed.' Miss Kind takin a Tom over on bed. Gettin on bed. On it it is a man a Paul Pot. 'Are you Paul Pot.'

Paul Pot noddin.

'Tom stay on the bed.' Miss Kind sayin it holdin on shoulders of Tom.

Me pointin at door. 'There aint a party.'

'There is a party Tom.'

Paul Pot sayin: 'Tom those sweeties you swallowed. Theyre tablets. They make you imagine things.'

Miss Kind noddin. 'Every things normal really isnt it Paul.'

Paul Pot noddin.

'Is everythin imagine then.'

Miss Kind noddin.

Paul Pot sayin: 'If we all stay on the bed.'

Every one stayin on bed.

'This bed.' Miss Kind holdin on Tom sayin: 'Is a magic bed. When you close your eyes Tom. It floats out of the window and up in to the sky and soars over magical lands and cities.'

Me shuttin a eyes.

Robert Tablet

In my class. There is a boy in my class. He aint even in it he is in a shop a toy shop.

I am in toy shop. Havin a look at toys. There is a ones called Orange Men. They are. Men made of oranges. Not real oranges a plastic oranges a orange orange shape. It is got arms an a legs an orange shape head fruit head. It is got on it a eyes a face. They are the same ones got difrent trouser. It is the ones what you can get.

Me pickin up a Orange Men holdin it in a box pack legs pokin out a bottom. On it it says: Eat more oranges. I am holdin it lookin round shop at a people what are in it. Then. There is a boy a tall boy he is in my class.

Me goin up to boy. He is called. Big Ben. He is the tallest boy in the world it is in a world book of records. He is nine but. He is taller than a groan up even a tall groan up standin on a toys.

Tall groan up sayin at Big Ben sayin: 'Excuse me sir could you reach up and fetch that—'

Big Ben lookin down at tall groan up.

'O. I thought—'

Big Ben shakin head.

Me goin up to tall groan up. 'He is a boy,' I say. 'It is in a record book of records.'

Tall groan up lookin at me gettin con fuse.

Me holdin up hand doin shape of tall.

Big Ben shakin head. Not sayin nothin. He is tall too tall. Dont say nothin if you are tall too tall.

'Well would you mind passing me that toy. The one with the gun thing.'

'He is in a book,' I say. 'He is. The tallest boy in the world. Every one calls him Big Ben.' Me pointin at Big Ben sayin it.

'The next one.' Tall man sayin: 'With the double laser cannon thing.'

Big Ben gettin toy. Givin it to that man. Man sayin thank you lookin con fuse goin a way. Big Ben lookin at me sayin: 'I hate being tall.'

'No,' I say lookin up at Big Ben. 'It is good it is. Bein tall is.'

Big Ben shakin head. Lookin at floor.

'It is,' I say.

'How would you know.'

'Im little.'

'How can you know about being tall. If youre not tall.'

'If you are tall,' I say lookin up at Big Ben. 'It means. You aint little.'

Big Ben makin tall face. 'You dont have to be tall to be not little. You just have. You just have to be not little.'

'Whats your best Orange Men.'

'What are Orange Men.'

Me holdin on Big Ben trouser leg knee cap. Pullin Big Ben over at a Orange Men. 'You should get it,' I say holdin it a Orange Men. 'Tell your mum to get it.'

'Im not allowed toys.'

Me laughin at joke. Big Ben doin joke.

'Its not funny. Its horrible. Not having toys.'

'Why aint you allowed toys then.'

'Mum says Im too tall. I get stupid adult things instead. Ties and things. Socks.'

'I get a socks,' I say holdin up a leg feet shoe.

'Not for your birthday. For your big present.'

'I dont even get a big present,' I say. 'I aint even got a mum an a dad.'

Big Ben takin down a Orange Men. Lookin down. At me. 'Where are they then. Your mum and dad.'

'My dad.' Me thinkin. What I am goin a say. 'He is in space. On a space ship.'

Big Ben makin face.

'My mum. I have got a new one a new mum.'

'What happened to the old one.'

'Killed.'

Big Ben noddin.

'What one do you want,' I say. 'If you are allowed.'

Big Ben lookin at Orange Men. 'Arent they all the same.'

Me pointin at trousers. 'Difrent trousers.'

Big Ben noddin.

'You can take em off look.' Me pullin down a trousers of a Orange Men showin a Orange Men willy a banana it is orange. 'You can swap em round. Put a difrent trousers on a difrent ones.'

166

'Whats the point. If theyre all the same.' Big Ben lookin at Orange Men two of em holdin em up next to be side sayin: 'If theyre the same. Identical. Whats the point in swapping the trousers.'

'Theyre difrent trousers.'

'But the actual Orange Men are the same. The actual figures.'

Me noddin.

'So why swap the trousers.' Big Ben holdin up a Orange Men. 'Why not just swap the Orange Men.' Big Ben holdin up a other one. Holdin in a hand one in each one. Then. Swap em put it in a other hand.

'Look,' I say pointin at Orange Men. 'It is still got a same trousers. You just moved it.'

'No but look.' Big Ben puttin Orange Men on shelf. There is a lot of em on it all the ones what you can get. Big Ben pointin at em. 'Look. Orange Men. This one has orange and red trousers and this one has red and orange trousers. Now watch this.' Big Ben gettin one of Orange Men one with a orange an red trouser on. Move a other one got a red an orange trouser on. Move it on a shelf takin it off shelf. Move it a long. Then. Put it on shelf. 'Look you see.'

Me shruggin.

'You see what I did.'

'Moved em.'

'Yes.' Big Ben says: 'Effectively swapping the trousers.'

Me shakin head. Pointin. At a Orange Men trousers. 'It is still got. Orange an red trousers.'

'Red and orange trousers.'

Me shruggin. 'Its the same.'

'Thats what I mean. Theyre the same figures. If you. If you swap the trousers. You end up with the same.'

Me noddin.

'So whats the point.' Big Ben pointin at Orange Men gettin cross. 'So whats the point in swapping the trousers. Whats the point.'

'Its toys.'

Big Ben shakin head.

'Dont you like toys.'

'I dont think I under stand them.'

'Ask your mum,' I say. 'If you can get a toys.'

'I did ask her. I wanted Richard Rubbish Bin and Richard Rubbish Bag action figures. For my birthday.'

'Did you get it.'

Big Ben shakin head. Big Ben holdin up a leg it is tall too tall. Pullin up a trouser leg. Showin a socks. 'Socks.'

Me noddin.

'Why havent you been at school Tom. You havent been for ages.'

'I have,' I say sayin it a fib.

'Then why. Then why havent I seen you.'

Me laughin. Hidin be hind hand. 'Im little. You are tall carnt see me if you are tall.'

Big Ben shakin head. 'You havent really been at school have you.'

Me shakin head.

'Is that because of your mum.'

'She is black a mum a black dad mum man a lady.'

Big Ben gettin con fuse.

'It is like.' Me thinkin. 'You know that world book of records. It is in a world book of records. It is. A worlds mummest man.'

Big Ben laughin.

'Can I get a Orange Men.'

'Dont ask me.' Big Ben says: 'Just because Im tall. Doesnt mean. Doesnt mean Im an adult.'

Me askin my dad askin Boxford. It is at that house got door broke. Me standin at door. I have runned home from toy shop. Me doin run Big Ben doin walk he is tall too tall. Big Ben waitin over a road. Me shoutin at door shoutin: Dad. Dad. Dad. Boxford comin down stairs dressed as a lady gettin a hump sayin: What. What. What. Me sayin: Can I get a Orange Men. Boxford sayin: No. No. No.

Me runnin up stairs. Boxford gettin out of way. Me runnin up findin Roxy sayin: 'Roxy can I get a Orange Men.'

'What are Orange Men.' Roxy pattin on lap.

'It is a toys. Every one at schools got em.'

'How would you know you havent been going to school. Which reminds me. On Monday.' Roxy strokin Tom head hair. 'You start back at school.'

Me makin face.

'So what are these Orange Men.'

'It is a toys. I aint got a toys. I am a kid but. I aint got a toys.'

Roxy strokin hair.

'All what I got is. A Poll Tax Clown a bear.'

'Hes a nice bear. And he loves you very much.'

'Can I get a Orange Men.'

Roxy not sayin. Roxy sayin: 'Tom who was that man I saw you talking to over the road.' It is a window Roxy lookin out of window. Over a road. It is Roxy an Boxfords bed room. Roxy makin in it a costumes. Roxy lookin out of window. 'Hes still there. I did teach you stranger danger didnt I.'

'He aint a man,' I say. 'He is a boy he is at my school.'

'But hes so tall.'

'He is. The tallest boy in the world.'

Roxy laughin.

'It is in a record of a world of books. It is. The tallest one you can get.'

Roxy laughin.

'Every one calls him Big Ben. Every one in my school.'

'Do you miss school Tom.'

Me noddin. Not even knowin I am goin a do that nod.

'Are you sure thats not a man Tom.' Roxy twitchin curtains look out of window. 'Hes dressed like an adult.'

Me jumpin up an down on Roxys lap. 'For his birthday. He gets socks an ties.'

'How ridiculous. Because of his physique. He shouldnt be forced to dress a particular way. I feel very strongly about this Tom. As you know it is an issue close to my heart.' Roxy puttin hand on heart it is black. 'What with my being a transvestite.'

'Whats a transvestite.'

'Tom you know what a transvestite is. A transvestite is. A man. Who dresses. As a woman.'

'Aint you a woman then.'

'Didnt you see my cock at the party. And my big hairy balls.'

'Aint you a lady then.'

'O I am a lady.' Roxy sayin it lady like sayin: 'You dont have to be a woman to be a lady.'

'Can I get a Orange Men.'

'It depends. How much. They cost.'

Me pointin at window road. 'Big Ben knows it.'

'Was Big Ben in the toy shop with you.'

Me noddin.

'And he knows how much these orange things cost. These Orange Men.'

Me noddin. 'I carnt remember a numbers.'

'Then lets go out. And ask him. And find out.'

Me standin up. Gettin off lap skirt dress.

Roxy standin up. Straighten lap skirt dress. Holdin a hand of Tom. Goin out of bed room. Tom goin out of bed room.

Boxford standin on landin. 'Tom who was that man I saw you talking to. Over the road.'

'Big Ben,' I say.

'Hes in Toms class.'

'Is he a teacher.'

'Hes a boy in Toms class. Hes a record breaker apparently.' Roxy sayin: 'The worlds tallest boy.'

Me noddin. Holdin up hand of tall.

Me an Roxy goin down stairs.

Boxford goin down stairs sayin: 'Now this I have to see.'

'He dont like bein tall,' I say. 'Every one sayin he is tall. Askin him a bout it a book of records.'

Roxy openin front door. 'Well he probably doesnt like being made a spectacle of.'

'Is he wearin a spectacles,' I say doin joke.

Roxy pickin me up holdin me up.

Me an Roxy an Boxford goin over road at Big Ben sayin hello. Roxy a man dressed as a lady. Boxford a man dressed as a lady.

Big Ben standin by tree. He is taller than a tree.

Me an Roxy an Boxford goin up to Big Ben. Roxy sayin: 'Is your name Ben.'

Big Ben noddin.

'Hello Ben. Im Roxy Toms mum.' Roxy holdin out a hand. It is hairy got on it nail polish it is red.

Big Ben lookin at hand.

'He dont do shake a hand,' I say sayin it to Roxy. 'He aint even a groan up.'

Roxy noddin.

Boxford laughin.

Roxy says: 'Tom wanted to ask you something didnt you Tom. About toys.'

'Orange Men,' I say sayin it. 'How much. They are.'

Big Ben lookin at me.

'How much.' Roxy says: 'Are they.'

Big Ben lookin at me. Not sayin.

'Ben you and Tom were at the toy shop together werent you.'

Big Ben noddin.

'And you looked at some toys. Orange Men.'

Big Ben noddin.

'Tom said you would know how much they cost.'

Big Ben noddin.

'Well do you know. How much.' Roxy says: 'They cost these Orange Men cost.'

Big Ben sayin it how much they cost sayin: 'Ninety nine ninety nine.'

Roxy noddin. 'Thank you.'

Me wavin at Big Ben sayin: 'Bye.'

Big Ben goin. He is tall too tall.

Boxford holdin on Big Ben leg top trouser top. Holdin on sayin: 'Hold on.'

Big Ben lookin at Boxford.

Roxy sayin: 'Ben this is Toms dad. His new dad.'

Big Ben lookin down at Boxford.

'Tom tells us youre a record breaker.'

'Box dont embarrass him.'

'Its alright Roxy he doesnt mind. You dont mind do you

Ben. Youre a big boy now arent you Ben.' Boxford sayin he is a big boy sayin: 'I just wanted to ask if youre really a record breaker. Are you really a record breaker Ben. The tallest boy. In the world.'

Big Ben noddin.

'And. Are you tall all over.'

Roxy holdin on arm of Boxford pullin a way. 'We have to go now Ben.'

'Its alright.' Boxford sayin: 'He doesnt mind. You dont mind do you Ben.'

Big Ben shakin head.

'How far.' Boxford holdin on Big Ben finger hand. 'From finger to thumb.' Boxford lookin at finger an thumb gap. 'Wow. No wonder they call you Big Ben.'

Roxy an Boxford havin a talk. It is pocket money talk. Me askin for pocket money. Roxy sayin they are have a talk a pocket money talk a bout pocket money. Roxy an Boxford goin out of room. Out on up an down stairs. Havin talk.

Me sittin in Roxy an Boxfords bed room.

Roxy an Boxford out on stairs. Havin talk.

Me stand up get off bed. It is got on it costumes on it not even finish. One of em got a head shape of a animal a stress ape. One of em got a cloak blanket got diamonds on it doin sparkle. Me gettin off em gettin off bed. Open door have a look.

O.

Roxy lookin at me sayin: 'Tom.'

Me put head back in shut door get told off.

There is a bed got on it costumes. Got on it a Tom.

Door openin Roxy an Boxford comin in.

Roxy sittin on chair. Pattin on lap.

Me sittin on lap.

Boxford lookin at me sayin: 'Tom.'

Roxy sayin: 'Tom. Weve had a talk. And this is what weve come up with.'

Me noddin. Gettin a pocket money a Orange Men.

Boxford sittin on side of bed edge. On a costumes monkey stress ape head. 'Tom youre a big boy now.'

'Youve been thru a lot in your short life.'

'And we want you to be financially independent.'

'Good parents wouldnt hand you everything on a plate would they Box.'

Boxford shakin head. On ape head.

'Good parents teach their children how to develop and grow. We want to teach you. How to develop.' Roxy says: 'And grow.'

Boxford noddin.

'We want to teach you. How to generate your own in come. Isnt that right Boxford.'

Boxford noddin sayin: 'Give a boy a fish.'

'Uncle Dustman gaved me a fish.'

'Well this is part of the problem.' Boxford says: 'He should have given you a rod.'

'We want to teach you. Or rather. We want Robert to teach you. How to generate your own in come.'

Me smilin.

'Tom youre a very lucky boy.' Roxy holdin me liftin me up an down bouncin up an down on a lap doin it excited a lucky boy. 'Box give Robert a call.'

'Shall I tell him—'

Roxy shakin mud hair head. 'Just get him to come round.'

Boxford goin out of bed room.

'Now Tom.' Roxy sayin: 'Now Tom. Tom you remember

those sweeties you ate at the party. That made you go funny.
For a bout a week'

Me noddin.

'They were fun.' Roxy sayin: 'Werent they.'

Me noddin.

'And we know how much you like fun.'

'I like fun,' I say smilin. 'Its fun.'

Roxy noddin. Holdin on side of Tom. 'Do the children at
your school like fun Tom.'

Me noddin.

'Tom how would you like to help the children at your
school have fun. And. At the same time. Generate an in
come. Generate. Some money. Some spending money. Some
spends.'

'Orange Men money.'

'Orange blue what ever.'

'There aint a Blue Men,' I say. 'It is orange fruit. Blue aint
even a fruit.'

'Blue berries. The point is its your money and you can in
vest it how ever you see fit.'

'In vest it.'

'In a vest.' Roxy sayin: 'In your pants and vest.'

Me gettin off lap. Takin off trousers an a jumper top. Takin
off a socks. Runnin round room. In a pants an vest. Runnin
round room fall over muck a bout.

'Tom.'

'I am get a Orange Men.'

'I thought youd be pleased. But Tom you dont know what
Im asking you to do yet.'

'To do.'

'To generate an in come.'

'O.'

'Put your things on Tom.'

Me puttin on a things.

Roxy pattin on lap.

Me sittin on lap of Roxy it is black.

'Now Tom. You remember Robert Tablet. The one you thought was Father Christmas.'

'He is got a red beard.'

'Red hair. He hasnt got a beard.'

'Why is Robert Tablet called Robert Tablet.'

'Tablet is his name. And Robert because he sells tablets.'

'What tablets.'

'The sweeties. The sweets.'

'Are they tablets.'

Roxy noddin.

'Is that why they made me go funny.'

Roxy noddin.

'Will they make the children at my school go funny.'

'Not as funny as you went Tom. You went so funny you saw clowns. You went so funny. Its funny. We thought you were never coming back.'

Me laughin. Memberin.

'But you did come back didnt you.'

Me noddin.

'Mostly. Any way you ate too many. Spangles are fine if you dont eat too many.'

'Am I got a eat it.'

'You sell them. You and Robert Tablet. You are going to be. Roberts right hand man.'

'Am I a man.'

'Boy.' Roxy touchin hand touchin boy. 'Roberts right hand boy.'

*

Me standin out side school. It aint even Monday. It is Friday a last day of school. On Monday. I have got a go a school.

Me standin out side school. Puttin hand on school gate wall. Lookin at school.

Then.

Boy comin out of school. It is after a noon. It is a boy. He aint in my class. He is walkin up school path up to a gate got a uniform on.

Boy comin out of gate.

Me standin at gate. Lookin at boy.

Boy lookin at me sayin: 'What.'

Me not sayin.

'What you lookin at.'

'I am lookin at school,' I say lookin at school doin point a finger pointin the finger.

Boy noddin.

'What day is it to day it is.'

'Today.' Boy lookin at watch wrist shape. 'Today. Todays Friday.'

'On Monday. I have got a go a school.'

Boy noddin.

Boy walkin off.

Me lookin at school. Puttin hand on school gate wall.

Two boys comin out of class. Walkin a cross grass. One of boy pushin other boy muckin a bout. Other boy fallin on grass gettin grass green on school uniform it is spring. Other boy muckin a bout doin fight.

Me standin at gate. Boys walkin up to gate. One of em sayin: 'What you lookin at.'

Other boy lookin at me pointin at a Tom. 'Ive seen you. Youre in Miss Kinds class.'

Other boy sayin: 'Do you know Andrew Hand.'

Other boy sayin: 'You aint been at school for ages.'

Me noddin. Smilin. Doin it proud sayin: 'I have been on holler day.'

'Aint you comin back to school.'

'On Monday,' I say puttin hand on gate.

'I wouldnt if I were you.' One of boys says: 'Youre goin to get told off. Big time.'

'Miss Kind wont tell me off,' I say wipin hand spring on tee shirt. 'She is nice she is. Miss Kind is.'

'Miss Kinds left. Shes havin a baby.'

Me smilin. 'There aint a teacher then. I aint even got a go a school.'

'Theres a new teacher.' Boy lookin at boy. 'Whos that new teacher. Andrew Hands class.'

'Mister Stricter.'

'Thats it Mister Stricter.' One of boys sayin: 'Mister Stricter his name is. Hes strict an hes got a beard.'

Me makin face. Dont like it.

'Hes built like a door.'

'Hes got a mos tosh.'

'He used to work in an all boys school.'

'He hates boys.' One of boys sayin: 'He only likes girls.'

'He supports capital punishment.'

'Hes got this brief case made out of an alligator. Its still got the legs on.'

'He whacks you with a ruler.'

'He buggered some one up.'

'He tells you off for runnin in the corridor. When you aint even runnin.'

'Hes got a really loud voice.'

'He shouts.'

'You can hear him shoutin all the way down the corridor.'

'He makes you do five hundred lines.'

'When you have swimming. If you forget your trunks. He makes you do it in the nude.'

'He laughed at Andrew Hands willy.'

'Thats the only time hes ever laughed. Ever.'

'If you laugh. You have to share the joke. With the class.'

'You have to tie your own shoe laces.'

'Hes wanted by the police.'

'He used to kill people.'

'You dont even have to be in his class.'

'Dont run in the corridor. He trips you up.'

'He cracked some ones head open.'

'You have to keep your hands on the table.'

'He comfy skates everythin. He comfy skated Andrew Hands Orange Men.'

'He hates Orange Men.'

'Hes got a whole cubberd full of Orange Men.'

'He banned Orange Men from the school.'

'He eats sand witches with his mouth full.'

'He wears brown trousers.'

Them boys sayin it. Sayin all that what is Mister Stricter.

One of boys sayin: 'Are you scared.' Pointin at me sayin at other boy sayin: 'Hes scared of Mister Stricter.'

Me not sayin nothin. Puttin hand on wall. On school wall. Not goin a school.

'If you miss too much school.' One of boys sayin: 'They put you in Behind Class.'

'Whats Behind Class,' I say.

'Its a special class for lepers. With special knees.'

Me lookin at knees. 'Have I got a special knees.'

Boy noddin.

179

Other boy noddin.

Me wipin a eye. Doin cry.

That boy. He is got a Orange Men. Me goin round his house play a Orange Men.

Other boy goin home sayin: 'Im goin home see ya.'

Me an boy walkin on grass. Boy got a can of fizzy. Openin can of fizzy doin drink.

'Whats your name.'

'Nathan.'

Me noddin.

'Youre Tom aint you.'

Me noddin. I am Tom I aint got a fizzy.

Me an Nathan walkin on grass. It is spring in park a way thru to Nathans house. Nathan walkin home from a school got a school uniform on me not got it on it aint even Monday.

Me an Nathan walkin on grass. It is got a poo on it what a doggy did. Nathan jumpin over poo landin on it gettin poo on shoe. Wipin it on grass. Me walkin round poo not gettin it on shoe it is a smell a smell of poo.

'Have you seen that new poo toy.'

Me shakin head.

'Its tops. Big time.' Nathan holdin out hands doin shape of holdin poo. 'My mum hates it. Its this brown stuff an you make difrent poos with it. It smells like real poo.'

'Whats it called.'

'Poo.'

Me noddin.

Me an Nathan doin walk.

'How many Orange Men you got.'

'Ten.'

'Ten.'

Nathan noddin.

Me not sayin nothin. He is got a ten Orange Men.

Me an Nathan doin walk.

Me sayin: 'Im gettin one for my birthday.'

'What one you gonna get.'

Me shruggin. There is difrent ones. You can get.

'Get the one with the orange trousers.' Nathan jumpin over poo. Nathan sayin: 'Its the tops.'

'Can you really get one with orange trousers.'

Nathan noddin.

'What colour is the Orange Men figure,' I say. 'The actual figure.'

'Orange. Theyre all orange. Or they aint official genuine Orange Men.'

'Carnt you get a Blue Men.'

'Only in Taiwan. But they aint official genuine Orange Men.' Nathan takin off tie. Roll it in shape of pie. Put it in pocket a pie tie pie. It is hot it is spring near a end.

Me lookin up at sky. It is got a cloud in it shape of a Orange Men. Me pointin up at sky. At cloud.

Nathan lookin up at cloud. Laughin. 'Tops.'

'Wheres your house.'

Nathan pointin at house at back of it. It is a back of park at back of house.

'You live near the park.'

Nathan noddin.

Nathan openin gate back gate. Goin in gate.

'Is your mum in,' I say goin in gate.

Nathan shakin head. 'We can play with the poo toy.'

'Tops,' I say sayin it like Nathan sayin it.

Nathan walkin thru garden me walkin thru garden. Nathan steppin over bike it is broke. Me walkin round bike.

181

Look at a climb frame it is broke got under it carpet purple. Nathan openin back door me an Nathan goin in back door goin in hall got same carpet it is purple got string bits.

Me an Nathan in house in hall. Me lookin at carpet. It is got on it a poo a toy.

'Do you want some fizzy.'

Me noddin.

Nathan goin in kitchen pour a fizzy.

Me pickin up poo toy. Smellin it it smells.

Nathan comin out of kitchen got a fizzy drink straws.

Me holdin poo toy.

Nathan makin face. 'That aint the poo toy. Thats poo.'

Doggy come out of front room sayin: 'Woof.'

Me an Nathan goin round house of Big Ben. Me tellin Nathan a bout Big Ben sayin: 'Have you seen him.'

'What. At school.'

Me noddin.

'Whats he look like.'

'He is tall he is. He is,' I say. 'A tallest boy in a world.'

'Tops.'

'He is got a tall house. He is got.' Me sayin it a fib sayin: 'A light house.'

'Tops.'

'He is got. A tree dad tall as a tree made of tree.'

Nathan laughin. 'Tops.'

Me an Nathan walkin round a corner road. Walkin up to a house.

Nathan lookin at house. 'Its a normal house.'

Me noddin.

'Didnt you say its like a tree house or somethin.'

'A light house.'

'Yeah a light house.'

Me noddin. Press a door bell it is normal.

Me an Nathan waitin.

Me lookin up at sky it is up an blue.

Me lookin at door.

Door openin a dad doin a open. It is a normal dad not even made of a tree. Normal dad sayin: 'Are you friends of Ben.'

Me doin nod.

Dad goin an get a Ben a Big Ben.

Nathan lookin at me makin face sayin: 'I thought you said his dad was like a light house.'

'A tree,' I say sayin.

Nathan noddin.

Then. In a door. It is a boy he aint got a head.

Boy bendin showin head pokin it under a door frame brick wood he is got a head.

Nathan laughin.

Big Ben a tallest in a world in a house a normal house lookin out of house sayin: 'Hello Tom.'

'Are you playin out,' I say sayin it.

Big Ben lookin at boy what is Nathan got a Orange Men holdin it be hind back doin hide it a sir prize. Big Ben sayin: 'Im not allowed to play out. Im not allowed to play.'

Nathan sayin: 'Can we come in your house.'

Big Ben lookin in house. Big Ben lookin at dad. Then. Lookin out of house sayin: 'Alright. But not to play. We have to behave like adults.'

Me noddin.

Nathan doin a face. Not doin play.

Me an Nathan goin in house. Goin up a stairs a normal stairs doin it normal. Big Ben goin up stairs not doin it normal he aint normal.

In bed room. It aint even for kids. It is a groan up bed room got a big bed for groan ups got on it flowers a mums. Got a war drobe shut aint got a toys.

Big Ben sittin at desk.

Nathan lookin at desk at Big Ben sayin: 'Are you doin your home work.'

Big Ben shakin head. Big Ben sayin it what he is doin sayin: 'Im filling in my tax return.'

Nathan doin face.

Me an Nathan sittin on bed.

Big Ben doin taxi turn.

Me an Nathan sittin on bed.

Big Ben turnin head.

Me an Nathan sittin on bed. Smilin.

Big Ben turnin head not doin a taxi turn turnin head sayin: 'Why are you smiling.'

'We have got.' Me doin nudge shape on elbow arm of Nathan. 'A. Orange Men.'

Nathan got a Orange Men be hind back showin it to Big Ben.

Big Ben droppin pen. Open a mouth a train comin.

Nathan throwin it Orange Men at Big Ben.

Big Ben catchin it droppin it not doin a catch not even a kid. Pickin it up hold it on lap look at it. 'What do you do with it.'

'You play with it.'

'I havent played with toys since I was a tall baby. If Dad sees it.' Big Ben standin hittin head on roof. 'He will hit the roof. I dont know what to do with it. What do I do with it.'

'You play with it.' Nathan sayin it shruggin sayin: 'Adventures.'

'What sort of adventures.'

Nathan lookin round a room a groan up bed room. Lookin for a adventures. Lookin up at curtain rail top pointin at it sayin: 'The top of the curtain. That could be a cable car or somethin.'

Big Ben lookin down at curtain rail top. Big Ben puttin Orange Men on curtain rail top. Standin back lookin down at it it is a long way down.

Me an Nathan sittin on bed.

Big Ben lookin at toy doin play a adventure.

Me an Nathan sittin on bed. Foldin a arms.

Big Ben sayin: 'Whats happening now.'

'Thats it.' Nathan says: 'Youre playin.'

Big Ben smilin lookin at play sayin: 'I like it. Its fun.'

It is fruit in a fruit box of fruit. Boxford bringin in fruit box of fruit. It is a special box of fruit box a crate. Boxford got crate put it on bed.

Roxy sittin on chair at desk. Makin a costumes.

Me sittin on desk Roxy said Im allowed. It is got on it. Sew it machine. Cup of tea. Costumes. Tom.

Boxford puttin crate on bed.

Roxy turnin. Lookin at crate box of fruit. Lookin at Boxford. 'Whats with the fruit.'

'What fruit.'

Roxy pointin at fruit box crate on bed.

Boxford not sayin. Boxford goin down stairs.

Me an Roxy listenin Roxy sayin: 'Shh.'

Boxford foot steps comin up stairs. Boxford comin in got fruit box of fruit a crate a other one. Put it on bed. On other one other crate box.

'Box.' Roxy says: 'Whats with the fruit.'

'Which fruit.'

Roxy pointin at fruit.

Boxford not sayin. Goin down stairs.

Roxy sayin: 'Hes up to something.'

Boxford comin up stairs. Got a crate box of fruit. Put it on bed. Go down stairs. Comin up stairs. Got a crate box of fruit. Put it on bed. Then. Shuttin door. Sit on bed get breath back.

'Box.' Roxy says: 'Whats with the fruit.'

'Which fruit.'

'The fruit the fruit.'

'Yes but which actual fruit.'

Roxy pointin at boxes of fruit gettin cross sayin: 'The fruit Boxford the fruit.'

'This fruit.' Boxford lookin at fruit. 'This fruit is for the play.'

'Play.'

Boxford noddin.

'Youre in a play.'

Boxford noddin. Smilin. Grinnin doin it black got white teeth.

'What about theatre school.'

'Thats in the autumn. This is the summer run. At the Icy Eh.'

'Youre in a play.'

Boxford noddin.

Roxy standin up smilin doin hug.

Boxford standin up smilin doin hug same one.

Me jump off desk on Boxfords back on back of hug.

Every one gettin excited. Boxford gettin fruit doin hungry juggle. Me gettin fruit look at fruit it is a fruit. Roxy eatin apple fruit give Boxford a kiss. Me laughin. Eatin a sweets it is in pocket fruit flavour sweets.

186

'What sort of play.' Roxy says: 'Whats it about.'

'Its um. Your classic fish out of water tale. With a political bent.'

Roxy lookin at fruit. 'And what is this play called.'

'Lord of the Fruit Pies.'

Roxy sittin on bed. 'O.'

Boxford sittin on bed next to be side Roxy in front of fruit crate box piled up put arms round a Roxy. 'Its not as bad as it sounds.'

'Is it a comedy.'

Boxford shakin head.

'So its actually worse than it sounds.'

Boxford noddin.

'Whats the plot. What actually happens.'

Boxford holdin out hands. Doin shape of plot of theatre curtains a play. 'Cargo plane. Crash lands on a deserted island. The only surviving food stuffs—'

Roxy laughin.

'The only surviving food stuffs are twenty six assorted fruits and vegetables. One of the fruits the apple I think—'

'Ive just eaten the apple.'

'There are other apples Roxy.'

Roxy spittin out pip. 'We should hold an audition.'

'Roxy this is serious.' Boxford sayin it serious got a hump sayin: 'Now where was I.'

'The apple.'

'The apple. Stumbles a cross a toy trumpet. He blows this trumpet to summon the other—'

'I think I know where this is going.' Roxy standin up. Walkin round room. Makin shape of play. 'These food stuffs. Over a period of time. Be come less and less to resemble whole some fruits and vegetables. And degenerate. In to mouldy savages.'

Boxford noddin. 'Its rotten isnt it.'

Roxy noddin.

Boxford an Roxy laughin.

Me sittin laughin jumpin on lap of Boxford an Roxy.

Roxy lookin at fruit. 'I feel sorry for them now.'

Boxford laughin.

'So these are the actual fruit.' Roxy askin it sayin: 'I hope theyre classically trained.'

'The fruits are played by human actors. I bought these for inspiration.'

'You need inspiration.'

'Not for me for you.' Boxford says: 'The costumes.'

Roxy raisin a eye brow mud flaps. 'Am I making the costumes.'

'The regular costume designer is allergic to sucrose.'

Roxy laughin. 'We do need the money.'

'So youll do it.'

Roxy noddin. Laughin.

Boxford gettin fruit box crates. Gettin lid off gettin out a fruit. 'The way it works is. The cast. Its alphabetical.' Boxford gettin fruit out of boxes. Sayin what it is sayin a fruit alpha bet sayin: 'The apple youve already devoured.'

'And very inspiring it was too.' Roxy sayin it pattin tum.

'B is for banana. Thats me.'

Roxy fallin on floor carpet doin laugh.

'I play a perfectly good banana. I debuted as a banana in the school play.'

Roxy sittin up. Laughin. Got a cry in a eye.

'C is for colly flower. D is for duck. Not strictly a fruit that one.' Boxford openin crate duck come out of crate walk out of crate doin quack.

Roxy turnin crawlin out of door got costume on on head.

'Its alright hes a perfect gentle man. Arent you Gilbert.'

'Quack.'

Roxy comin in room. Hidin be hind door. Laughin.

Duck got try angle shape feet sayin: 'Quack.'

Roxy laughin.

'E is for egg fruit.'

'Again not strictly a fruit.'

'O it is Roxy.' Boxford says: 'It not part egg part fruit as the name might suggest. Its a fruit look. Its the fruit of the egg plant.'

'It looks like an ober jean.'

'It is an ober jean.' Boxford got it it is purple an big an got green hat on it is happy. 'Egg plant is its pseudonym. Its nom de plumb. Any way F is for fennel.'

'Which I hate with a passion.'

'What sane person doesnt. G is for grapes. As in bunch of. H is for haricot a member of the bean family. I is for idiocy.'

'We know all about that.'

'J is for jack o lantern. A sort of haunted pumpkin. Ive got the recipe some where. You take a regular pumpkin. Hollow it out and carve the mouth and eyes.'

Roxy goin in kitchen. Gettin knife.

'K is for kumquat. How ridiculous. Why they couldnt have gone for the kiwi fruit. With its fuzzy brown skin and green flesh. I will never know. L is for lime.' Boxford holdin up lime. 'Or is it an under ripe lemon. M is for mango.'

'The feminists favourite.'

'Quite. N is for nectarine. The smooth skinned peach. With the hard centre. O is for orange.'

Orange. Orange Men.

'P is for pine apple the edible punk rocker. Q is for quince. Never even heard of that one.'

'It looks like pear.'

Boxford sayin it sayin what it is sayin: 'Its a quince. They call it the fools pear. R is for radishes. S is for star fruit my personal favourite. You dont need to eat it to enjoy it just hang it from the ceiling on a length of cotton.'

Roxy gettin cotton. Hangin it up.

'T is for tulip. Oddly.' Boxford lookin in box crates findin it a fruit a tulip flower it is red. 'U is for ugli fruit. Do not miss spell. For fear of causing offence.'

Roxy laughin. Laughin at fruit an Boxford got a fruit.

'V is for voacanga root bark. Yes there is such a thing.' Boxford holdin it a such a thing. 'It may look like manure. But believe me it tastes like shit. Water melon we are all familiar with. X is for xigua.' Boxford holdin it bitin it is round purple got in it pink. 'If any fruit tastes like paradise. Its the xigua.'

'Let me try.'

Boxford givin it fruit drip bits to a Roxy.

Roxy eatin it. Noddin. Smilin.

'Y is for yam. I thought a yam was an animal but apparently not.'

Roxy holdin yam take it out of Boxford hand. 'Thats no animal Box.' Roxy pointin at duck. 'Thats an animal.'

'Quack.'

Roxy an Boxford laughin sayin at duck sayin: 'Quack quack quack.'

'Quack.'

'Z is for zucchini. Which is this green penis like object here. More commonly known as the summer squash. And thats it all twenty six.'

'And I have to make a costume for each. Each of these fruits and vegetables.'

'Quack.'

'And the duck.'

Duck noddin.

Boxford noddin. 'Dress rehearsals begin in two weeks. So you had better get your sewing skates on.'

If I dont go a sleep. I aint got a wake up go a school.

Me goin in Roxy an Boxford bed room sayin: 'If I dont go a—'

O.

Roxy lookin at me sayin: 'Shit.'

Boxford sayin: 'Shit. Roxy I really did not want Tom to see us in this position.'

Me goin out. Shuttin door.

Roxy comin out openin door comin out sayin: 'Tom youve seen it now you might as well come in.'

Me goin in.

Roxy is makin banana costume for theatre for Boxford in play. Boxford wearin banana costume it is yellow. Roxy sewin it up measurin it up. Boxford sittin on bed edge. Got a banana costume a banana.

'Tom.' Roxy says: 'Tell me honestly. What do you think.'

Me in pants an a vest standin pointin sayin: 'He looks like a banana.'

Roxy smilin. Sit on chair at desk. 'That was the desired effect.'

Boxford sayin: 'Im not peeling very well. I think I need to lie down.'

'You will do no such thing. Ive got to make twenty six of these bloody costumes.'

Boxford unpeelin peel. 'I hope youre not expecting me to model for all twenty six.'

'Well Tom carnt do it. Hes too small.'

Me noddin doin it small.

Boxford unzippin zip. 'Well Im not bloody well doing it.'

'O please Boxford.'

Boxford unpeelin zip. 'Hire a model.'

Boxford Im not being paid much as it is. If I hire a model—'

Boxford unzippin peel. 'Advertise for a fruit perver in the local paper. A grocery fetishist.'

'Thats not a bad idea.' Roxy says: 'I assume the actors are all the same size.'

'Hardly.' Boxford climbin out of banana costume steppin out wearin white banana in side costume bit. 'Some of them are over weight. The man who plays the orange is rotund.'

Orange Men.

'The radish woman is pencil thin.'

Roxy doin sigh. 'I will just have to make them adjustable. Tom shouldnt you be in bed. School tomorrow.'

'I aint goin a bed,' I say doin say. 'I aint goin a school.'

Roxy givin me look.

Boxford givin me banana look. Takin off white banana in side costume bit.

'Tom weve gone thru this.' Roxy says: 'You have to go to school. Every one has to go to school. Even ducks go to school dont you Gilbert.'

'Quack.'

'If you dont go to school. You wont learn lots and you wont earn lots of money. Youll end up working for Robert Tablet all your life. Or living in a dirty house like that boy you told me about. With the poo.'

'Its a toy,' I say holdin shape of toy. 'It is. The smelliest shape you can make.'

'Tom go to bed. No son of mine plays with poo. Or do you want a smack bum.'

Boxford sayin: 'That was a rhetorical question Tom you dont have to answer.'

Roxy lookin at Boxford. 'Whose side are you on.'

'Gilberts. We look after our own dont we Gilbert.'

'Quack.'

Roxy shakin head doin it cross. 'Boxford. Back in your costume. Tom. Bed.'

'Can I have a Orange Men.'

'If we buy you an Orange Men.' Roxy sittin on bed edge of bed. 'Will you go to bed.'

Me noddin.

Roxy smilin. Puttin hands on lap. 'Go on then off to bed.'

'Can I have a Orange Men.'

'Tomorrow.' Roxy sayin: 'Tomorrow you can have an Orange Men. Boxford will go to the toy shop first thing in the morning wont you Boxford. Dressed as a fruit salad.'

Boxford noddin. Puttin on trouser normal one. 'You can stuff the fruit salad part. But yes Tom you will have your toy. First thing in the morning. I will go to the shop. In my civvies.'

'It is open.'

Boxford lookin down at trouser zip. 'What is.'

'The toy shop.'

Boxford zippin up trouser zip.

Roxy doin sigh. 'Tom its the middle of the night.'

'Orange Men,' I say doin foot stamp doin it cross.

'Fine.' Roxy doin sigh a other one the same one. 'Boxford will pop down there now. Wont you Box.'

Boxford lookin at Roxy.

Me goin a bed.

*

Me in bed. In bed room. A wake.

Me lookin at ceiling. It is dark it aint a ceiling.

Me holdin Poll Tax Clown a bear. He is nice a best bear you can get. He is. My mum got it is nice a bear. Me thinkin it sleepy goin a sleep. Carnt think it the thinks goin funny fallin off.

Then. Door openin Boxford comin in sayin: 'Tom.'

Me sit up a wake.

Boxford turnin on light on. It hurtin eyes me shuttin eyes. Then. When I open a eyes. Boxford got Orange Men holdin it up sayin: 'Hey presto.'

Me lookin at Orange Men. It aint a Orange Men. It is. A orange.

Boxford lookin at me holdin orange. Showin me it a orange sayin: 'Orange Men.'

Me not sayin nothin.

Boxford comin in room. Got that orange it is a fruit orange out of fruit box fruit. Boxford walkin a cross floor got bare feet smell got a orange. Boxford holdin orange sayin: 'Here.'

Me shakin head.

'You wanted a sodding Orange Men and here it is a sodding Orange Men.'

'It aint one look.' Me pointin at orange.

'Its orange.' Boxford says: 'Its an Orange Men. Whats the difference.'

'It aint a man,' I say pointin. 'It aint got a face.'

Boxford lookin at orange. 'O. I see. Um.' Boxford doin think. 'There must have been a mix up at the toy shop. Back in five mins.' Boxford shuttin door. Boxford goin out of bed room shuttin door. Turnin off light off. Goin out. Shuttin door.

Me holdin on covers. Coverin up a Tom a Poll Tax Clown. In bed. In dark. Goin a sleep.

Then. Jus when I am goin a sleep. Door openin Boxford comin in.

Me sit up wake up. 'Have you got my Orange Men.'

Boxford turnin on light on. It hurtin eyes me closin eyes doin eye rub. Sittin up. Lookin at Boxford what he is got. Boxford holdin up what he is got sayin: 'Hey presto. Again.'

'What is it.'

'An Orange Men.' Boxford holdin up orange sayin: 'That orange they gave me. I returned it to the toy shop. Fortunately I had kept the receipt. They apologised for the mix up and replaced it with this an Orange Men action figurine.'

Me lookin at orange it is a orange got on it a face drawin on it a felt tip pen.

'Happy.'

Me shakin head.

'Youre not happy.'

Me shakin head.

'Youre un happy.'

Me noddin. Pointin at orange at un happy face.

'Its an Orange Men.'

'Its a orange,' I say pointin at orange.

'No look its a man.' Boxford pointin at face sayin: 'Its got a face.'

'You drawed it.'

'Did I.'

Me noddin.

'But its the same. Is it not. As the ones in the shop. As seen on TV.'

'It aint got a arms an a legs.'

'Arms and legs.'

Me noddin.

'Arms and legs.' Boxford sayin it goin out of room. Not turnin light off. Shuttin door.

Me under covers got Poll Tax Clown holdin tum. Holdin tum of Poll Tax Clown. It is a bare tum a bear a bare tum bear. Me holdin bear put it on Tom tum tum.

Then. Door openin Boxford comin in. Shakin head. Standin at door. Got it be hind a back.

Me sittin up.

Boxford got it be hind back a sir prize. Holdin it out of be hind back. Not even sayin a hey presto. Holdin a orange. It is got. Stick arms an stick legs. It is from kitchen a stick a dick it is left over from party.

Me lookin at orange. Doin face.

'What are you making that face for Tom.'

'Trousers,' I say pointin at legs aint got a trousers.

'Trousers.'

Me noddin.

'What sort of trousers.'

'Leg trousers. It is got difrent ones you swap it. Put a difrent trousers on. A difrent ones,' I say. 'You can get.'

Boxford doin sigh. Goin out of room. Shuttin door.

Me gettin out of bed.

Me sittin on bed.

Me look at bear.

Me standin up.

Me openin door. Goin out. Goin a find a Boxford.

At Boxford an Roxy bed room door. Listenin. At door.

It is a noise a sew it machine.

Then. Door openin me runnin runnin in bed room in pants an vest shuttin door get in bed got light on.

Boxford openin door. Pokin head round door. 'Tom.'

Roxy pokin head round door. 'Tom.'

Me sittin up. Doin pretend wake up.

Boxford an Roxy comin in.

Roxy sayin: 'Weve got a sir prize for you Tom. From the toy shop. The last one in the shop.'

Boxford noddin. Boxford got it be hind back. Boxford hold it out of be hind back. It is a Orange Men a real one got a arms an a legs an a face on it an a trousers a orange trousers. It is a orange trousers one a best one. You can get.

Oi oi my little girl

Me standin at door.

There is a teacher a lady. She is old she is got white hair an white shoes an a white dress got on it powder. She is got neck lace round neck got on it a metal point bit. She is a teacher a lady. Teacher lady lookin at Tom sayin: 'Are you our shiny new Tom.'

Me shakin head.

'Youre not Tom.'

Me noddin.

'You are Tom.'

Me noddin. I am Tom I am got special knees.

'Come in Tom.'

Me goin in. Walkin a way from door.

Me lookin round room. It is Behind Class. It is a big room got high up windows got a table it is big.

'Tom my name is Miss Dancer. I have never married. I

find husbands daunting.' Teacher lady sayin: 'Tom come and meet Stacy. Tom this is Stacy. Stacy. This is Tom.'

Me lookin at Stacy.

Stacy lookin at knees. She is little got special knees.

Miss Dancer standin in front of table sayin: 'Tom come and sit next to your new class mate.'

I am sit at table next to be side a girl she is little she is Stacy. She is the only children what is in the class there aint a other children in the class there aint a fun.

'Tom say hello to Stacy please.'

'Hello.'

Stacy pokin out tongue it is orange. She has eat a lolly.

'Stacy. Say hello to Tom.'

'Hello.'

Miss Dancer smilin. 'Now. Stacy. Give Tom a sniff.'

Stacy puttin nose next to be side that Tom. Doin sniff.

'Does he smell of poo.'

Stacy shakin head.

'So boys dont smell of poo.'

Stacy shakin head. They dont even smell of it.

Miss Dancer clappin hands got on it powder. 'Im glad we put that one to rest.' Miss Dancer got a chair at other side of table. Miss Dancer pull out that chair it is big. Sit on it put hand powder on table look at Stacy an Tom. Miss Dancer lookin at Tom sayin: 'Tell us why you are here Tom. Tell us why you are in Behind Class.'

'I didnt go a school.'

'You failed to attend school.'

Me noddin.

'You failed—'

I have got a say it. What she is sayin. Me sayin it what she is sayin sayin: 'I failed—'

'—to attend—'

'—to attend—'

'—school.'

'—school.'

Miss Dancer noddin.

'I didnt go it.'

Miss Dancer noddin. 'You have missed an awful lot of school Tom. And you need to catch up.'

Me noddin. Lookin at table top. It aint got a crayons.

'In fact. You have double catching up to do. Not only have you to catch up with your regular learning. You have to catch up with Behind Class too.' Miss Dancer smilin a teeth ache shape. 'Stacy has been attending Behind Class for several months. And you. Have only been attending Behind Class for.' Miss Dancer lookin at watch makin powder. 'Three minutes.'

Me noddin.

'Having said that. Stacy is two years your junior so in terms of maturity. You have the edge.' Miss Dancer openin drawer gettin out it a book. Not lookin at me talkin to me sayin: 'Behind Class is not as fun as normal class Tom.'

Me not sayin nothin. Not havin a fun.

'Having said that. There are few things more rewarding than catching up. Would you not agree Stacy.'

Stacy noddin.

'Having said that. Trying to catch up. By its very nature. Can be terribly frustrating. Like running after your parents. As they drive away. In a car. Never to return. Further more. There is no play time in Behind Class as Stacy knows only too well.'

Stacy noddin head. Doin grump.

Miss Dancer clappin a powder finger nail hand. 'To begin. Stacy have you got your Behind Book.'

Stacy holdin up book.

Miss Dancer got a book it is new. Miss Dancer puttin book on table hand it a cross table at a Tom. 'Tom. Write your name on the front. And the words. Behind Book. Stacy show Tom the front of your book.'

Stacy shuttin book. Showin front of book. On it on front of it it is got writ: Stacy Brain. Behind Book.

Me gettin a pen. Doin writin doin it neat my best hand writin writin: stacy bra—

'Tom. Tom what are you doing.'

Me look up at Miss Dancer.

'You put your name not Stacys name.'

Me doin cross out. Doin it neat my best cross out. Doin a writin. Doin it neat my best writin. Writin: tom boler. benin book.

'Good. We are now ready. To begin.' Miss Dancer sayin it fold a arms on table. Arms got powder on. Powder fallin off on table. Gettin powder on table. It is arm powder snow on table. Miss Dancer puttin arms on table. On arm powder. Gettin powder on a arms. Holdin up a arm. Brush it off it that powder that arm powder.

Stacy puttin her hand up sayin: 'Miss. What is that spike thing for.'

'This.' Miss Dancer lookin down at spike metal point bit. It is on a neck lace hang round a neck. 'This. This is a tooth pick. A silver queen anne anne teak tooth pick.' Miss Dancer holdin up that tooth pick put it in teeth. 'You pick your teeth with it.' Miss Dancer sayin it pick a teeth powder teeth.

Stacy makin face. She dont like it she is a kid she is nice.

Miss Dancer openin drawer. Gettin out a pen it is thick.

Shuttin drawer. Standin up sayin: 'To start.' Standin at white board. It is like black board but. White. Writin thick pen on it that white board writin: Logic.

Stacy lookin at word what it is. Stacy writin it in Behind Book writin: Logig.

Miss Dancer standin at white board at word. Lookin at a Tom. 'Tom. Do as is does done.'

Me makin face. Dont get it.

Stacy pokin me in a arm sayin it quiet sayin: 'You got a write it.'

Me openin Behind Book. Writin it writin: locig.

'Pens down.'

Me an Stacy puttin down a pen.

Miss Dancer got a pen drawin on white board. It is drawin of a animal a monkey. 'Tom.'

Me puttin hand up.

'You dont need to put your hand up Tom.'

Me puttin hand in Tom lap.

'Tom.' Miss Dancer tappin pen on white board a sound.

Me puttin hand up sayin: 'Miss. Its a monkey.'

'A monkey. Good.' Miss Dancer got lid off pen tappin on board next to be side monkey makin dots. Monkey lookin at dots gettin cross eyed cross sayin: Get off a dots. Monkey lookin at dots sayin it. Miss Dancer sayin: 'Do as is does done.'

Stacy lookin at monkey. Stacy lookin at Behind Book. Stacy drawin monkey in Behind Book.

Me drawin monkey in Behind Book.

'Pens down.'

Me an Stacy puttin down a pens.

Miss Dancer drawin a shape. It is a star shape a shape of star. Drawin it next to be side monkey. 'Stacy.'

Stacy sayin: 'A star.'

'A star. Good.' Miss Dancer holdin on pen lid. Miss Dancer lookin at me an Stacy. 'Do as is does done.'

Stacy drawin star in Behind Book.

Me drawin star in Behind Book.

'Pens down.'

Me an Stacy puttin down a pens.

'Now.' Miss Dancer drawin a nother star it is big. Drawin in it a monkey it is little it is in side star. 'What happens. If you put the monkey. In side the star.'

Me lookin at Stacy.

Stacy lookin at me.

Miss Dancer lookin at me. 'Tom.'

Me puttin hand up.

'You dont have to put your hand up Tom why are you putting your hand up.'

Me puttin hand in Tom lap.

Miss Dancer tappin on board sayin: 'Apply logic.'

Me puttin hand up sayin: 'It is in it.'

'The monkey is in side the star yes. But what do we get. What do we get when we put the monkey in side the star. Do as is does done. Draw it in your books.'

Me an Stacy drawin in it a books. Drawin a star it is big. Drawin a monkey it is little it is in side it.

'Apply logic. What do we get.' Miss Dancer tappin on board sayin it.

Me an Stacy lookin at Stacy an me.

Miss Dancer sayin it what we get sayin: 'Trouble.'

Stacy laughin.

Miss Dancer writin it on white board writin: Trouble.

Stacy writin it in book writin: Truoble.

Me writin it in book writin: truble.

'Pens down.'

Me an Stacy puttin down a pens. It is a learn it is logic.

'I have to pop out.' Miss Dancer sayin: 'For one minute. How many minutes is that Stacy.'

Stacy doin count on finger. Countin it on a finger.

'Stacy.' Miss Dancer sayin: 'How many minutes. Is one minute.'

Stacy holdin up a finger doin it rude put it up a nose nozzle nostle.

'One. Good. No talking I shall be back in one minute.'

Then. Jus when she is open it a door. Stacy puttin up hand sayin: 'Miss.'

Miss Dancer lookin at Stacy. 'Stacy yes.'

'Miss what if you dont come back.'

'I will come back. In one minute. Remain in your seats. Until I return.' Miss Dancer turnin door handle open a door.

Stacy puttin up a hand a other one other one is tired. 'Miss. Miss what if you dont come back. In one minute.'

'I will come back. If not in one minute.' Miss Dancer sayin: 'In two.'

'Miss what if you dont come back in two.'

'Stacy rest assured it will not be more than five. In any eventuality. Remain in your seats.'

'Miss what if youre not back in five. In five minutes.' Stacy sayin it standin up a bit but a bit in a seat. Stacy remain in in a seat sayin it sayin: 'How long have we got a remain in a seats.'

'Until I return.'

'But. What if you get killed.'

Miss Dancer laughin. 'Nothing is going to happen Stacy. Im a teaching professional. Have been for the past ninety years. I have simply to fetch something from the notice board. In the corridor. Back in five minutes max.'

'But what if youre not back in five hours. Or five years.'

Miss Dancer goin out of door. Shuttin door.

'Miss what if—'

'She is gone,' I say. 'She carnt even hear.'

Stacy foldin arms on table.

Me foldin arms on table.

Stacy lookin at me.

'What you lookin at me for,' I say lookin at Stacy for.

Stacy not sayin. She is stoopid a idiot a kid. Stacy gettin up sayin: 'Shall I have a look. See if she is comin.'

Me shakin head.

'She might of got killed.'

Me shakin head.

'Youre borin you are.'

'Im not.'

'You are.' Stacy says: 'If you aint muckin a bout you are.'

'Miss Dancer said no talkin.'

'So.'

'So,' I say tellin her off. 'You are get told off.'

Stacy laughin. Lookin at Behind Book at monkey it is rubbish aint even a monkey it is got a big bum tum a tum. Stacy lookin at monkey at me sayin: 'Show me your monkey.'

'No,' I say shuttin book. 'It will get a trouble.'

'Show me your monkey.'

Me showin Stacy that monkey it is little.

Stacy laughin. Laughin at me my monkey.

Me shuttin book.

Stacy gettin off chair goin over at a door doin it careful not gettin told off sayin: 'Shall I see if she is comin.'

Me not sayin nothin.

Stacy openin door. Look out of door.

'Is she comin.'

Stacy comin in shuttin door. Shakin head. She aint comin.

Me an Stacy in Behind Class. In seats. Remain in a seats.

Stacy puttin elbows on table.

Me foldin a arms.

Stacy pickin nose wipe it on table.

Me lookin at Behind Book.

Stacy doin noise a smell.

Me put hands in a pockets in uniform it is new. It is Roxy made it is rubbish got big pocket stitch.

Stacy pickin nose a other nose nozzle nostle.

Me foldin a arms.

Stacy standin up sayin: 'I am see if she is comin.' Walkin over at a door open door. Lookin out of door. Shuttin door doin it quick runnin sit on chair sayin: 'Shes comin shes comin.'

Me foldin arms.

Stacy foldin arms.

Me lookin at door.

Stacy lookin at door.

Me lookin at Stacy.

Stacy doin face grump one.

Me shruggin.

Stacy standin up doin dance walk walkin at door openin door lookin out of door.

'Is she there.'

'She is. She is got killed.'

Me shakin head. It is made up.

'She is layin in the corridor got blood on.'

Me shakin head.

'Its true.' Stacy lookin at blood sayin: 'She got runned over by a in door car.'

Me laughin. It is made up it is silly a joke.

'It aint a joke. Every one is got killed.' Stacy says: 'Have a look.'

Me shakin head.

'Go on have a look.'

'No,' I say. 'I will get told off.'

Stacy remain at door. Lookin out of door.

'Is she there.'

'Shes there shes dead.' Stacy makin it up sayin Miss Dancer is dead sayin: 'There is animals eatin Miss Dancer.'

'What animals,' I say.

'Lions. Tigers. Elephant ears.'

Me laughin.

'If you dont look. You carnt say it is a fib.'

'I aint sayin it is a fib.' I know it is a fib.

'Its true have a look.'

Me shakin head.

Stacy shuttin door. Stacy sittin in seat doin remain in a seat.

Me an Stacy openin door of cubberd. It is stock cubberd stock room. Stacy callin it sock room takin off socks open sock room cubberd door goin in cubberd.

It is got in it. Shelfs got paper on piled up. It is for cuttin out make an do. Books for writin aint got a writin. Pens in pen box. Pencils in pencil box got a rubbin out rubber on end a end of a world. Pencil sharpers in pencil sharpers box. Paper clips. Lastic bands.

At back of sock room. It is got. Cups. Paper clips. Knife an fork an spoon plastic holler days ones goin on holler day a pick nick eat it in a car. Pick nick paper plates. Stacy holdin a pick nick paper plates sayin: 'I want cake.'

'What sort of cake,' I say. 'Do you like.'

Stacy thinkin. Then. Makin shape of cake big one in a hands sayin: 'Big.'

Me laughin. She is funny a girl.

Then. Jus when she is made that shape. Stacy openin lid of box it is big it is on floor under bottom shelf dust. Openin lid. Lookin in box. It is a cake it is big.

Stacy lookin at me.

Me lookin at Stacy.

Stacy lookin at cake. Carnt believe a eyes. Carnt believe a cake. It is a cake it is big.

Stacy lickin lips. Lookin at cake.

'Its a cake,' I say lookin at cake. It is cake it is her best one it is big.

Stacy puttin finger in box touchin cake got it on finger.

'Dont. You will get told off.'

Stacy puttin finger in cake icing white cream top. Gettin it on finger. Put it in mouth. Lick it off fingers it is cake it is white sticky got on it.

Me goin back wards out of sock room stock room door.

Then. When I come out of stock room. There is a teacher a man. He is tall he is got a beard mos tosh. He is got a trousers it is green. Teacher man lookin at me sayin: 'Should you really be in the stock room.'

'There is a girl in it,' I say pointin.

'A girl.'

'She is got bare feet,' I say. 'She is bein naughty.'

Teacher man raisin a eye brow.

Teacher man goin in stock room sock room wearin brown socks an a shoes. Teacher man lookin in it. There is a girl in it. Teacher man goin in it sayin: 'Oi—'

Stacy lookin at teacher man. Got cake on face. Got cake on finger holdin it up it is rude.

'Where is Miss Dancer,' I say sittin in seat doin remain.

Teacher man not sayin. Teacher man goin in stock sock room. Teacher man shuttin door.

Me doin remain in a seat.

Me look at sock room stock room door. She is in it get told off. I carnt hear it that tell off.

Door openin Stacy comin out she is cryin.

Teacher man comin out. Not lookin at Stacy not lookin at me not tellin off goin out of class room shuttin door.

Stacy standin at sock room door.

Me lookin at Stacy.

Stacy not sayin nothin. Cryin.

'What you cryin for,' I say.

Stacy shakin head.

Me go in stock room got a socks on floor brush a dust off. Go out put it on a Stacy. Stacy cryin lift up a feet stink feet. Me put socks on feet sayin: 'Pull your socks up.'

Stacy doin pull a socks up.

Me an Stacy in seats. Remain in in a seats. Stacy sayin: 'Swap seats.'

Me shakin head.

Stacy doin stand up readin comic a stand up comic.

'Have you got a comic.'

Stacy shakin head. Put it hide be hind back a sir prize.

'Im not tellin you off,' I say not tellin off.

'You carnt tell me off you aint even a teacher.'

'Let me look then. If I aint tell you off. If I aint a teacher.'

Me reach out get a comic.

Stacy got comic holdin it turnin doin be hind read got a back to.

'Can I read it.'

Stacy shakin head. Got a back to. Readin a comic at window light it is spring shinin thru blue on comic.

Me lookin at door. Lookin at Miss Dancer but. She aint comin.

Me standin up. Have a look at comic.

It is called. Lorrence and the Shape. It is a boy it is Lorrence. Lorrence got a hair what is funny makin you laugh. He is got a shape a try angle. Lorrence holdin it a try angle. Lorrence throw it at a man hit on head knock a hat off. Man fallin over makin you laugh. Man standin up get a try angle it is on pavement. Man put it in pocket do comfy skate. Lorrence gettin up sayin: Thats mine.

Man shakin head.

Thats my try angle. Lorrence sayin: How can I create havoc. With out a try angle.

I dont want you to create havoc. Thats the point. Theres too much havoc in this world. Man sayin it got try angle in pocket shape of try angle not makin havoc.

Give me back my try angle. Lorrence sayin: Get your own try angle.

Man shakin head. Walkin off.

Lorrence thinkin. Doin a think. Think shape comin out of head a cloud. Thinkin: Hmm.

Lorrence walkin at man. Lorrence sayin: I wonder if the try angle is magic.

Man shakin head. Nonsense. No such thing.

Shake it. And see what happens.

Man shakin head. Man get try angle out of pocket. Shakin it sayin: See. Nothing happens.

Lorrence laughin makin you laugh.

Man shakin try angle shape. Doin shake shape shakin shape.

Then.

Magic comin out of try angle. It is stars an shapes an colour bits comin out of page. Stacy turnin page. Magic bits turnin page fillin up a page. Lorrence goin in magic. Lorrence in magic havin fun.

It is a only way of gettin a magic. You have got a get a shape shaked by a man. It is every week in comic a same. Lorrence got a shape a try angle. Lorrence throw it at a man or do trick with it or throw it at a woman a lady. Lady doin shake shapin that shake. Or. Dog doin it. Got it tied on tail a piece of string Lorrence tyin it on. Give dog present make it pleased make it wag a tail. Dog waggin it waggin shape. Doin tail wag shape shake doin it by mistake. Magic comin out of shape. Lorrence goin in magic. Lorrence goin a funny shape. Lorrence in magic havin fun.

Stacy shuttin comic.

Me an Stacy shakin head. Lookin at comic. Not lookin at it lookin a way.

Me an Stacy lookin at window.

Stacy puttin down comic. Doin grump shape face sayin: 'There aint a magic.'

Me shakin head. There aint it.

Me an Stacy sittin in seats remain in a seats.

Stacy sayin: 'Swap seats.'

'No we will get told off.'

'There aint even a teacher.'

'There is a teacher,' I say. 'Miss Dancer. She is comin back.'

Stacy shakin head.

Me an Stacy lookin at door it not openin Miss Dancer not comin back not comin in.

Stacy sayin: 'Swap seats.'

'We carnt we got a remain in a seats.'

'It is remain in a seats. It is.' Stacy sayin: 'Remain in a other seats.'

'What if Miss Dancer comes back. She will get a con fuse. If we are remain in a other ones.'

'If we swap seats. It will get a magic.' Stacy sayin it doin special shape face. Face sayin: There is there is there really is.

Me standin me an Stacy doin swap seats doin remain in a other seats a other one. Me sit in girl seat smells of sweets. Stacy sniffin boy seat it is smell of poo. Me an Stacy sittin in a other seats. Lookin at door it not openin Miss Dancer not comin in not get a con fuse not doin tell off.

In sock room stock room. Me an Stacy lookin in it. Lookin for a shape. Stacy takin off a socks put it out of stock room sock room. Sayin it is a sock room stock room you carnt wear a socks. Me goin in it sniffin feet it stinks. In it lookin for shape.

Stacy got comic holdin comic sayin: 'If we find a shape. We can make a magic.'

Me laughin. 'It aint real Stacy it is a comic.'

'It is real.' Stacy sayin: 'I saw it on telly.'

Me an Stacy goin in sock room stock room. Lookin for a shape.

Me lookin on shelf. At what is on it. It is. Knife an fork an spoon plastic holler day pick nick bits. Eat it on motor way on holler day on roof lid of car. Wavin at car it goin a way. Mum an dad drivin a way far a way goin a way gettin killed. Pick nick paper plates.

Stacy holdin a paper plates sayin: 'Plate shape.'

'Round,' I say movin finger makin shape of round. Say it a mouth makin shape of round.

Stacy lookin in comic. It is got in it. Lorrence. Got funny hair shape makin you laugh. Got shape. Holdin shape it is try angle. Stacy holdin plate shape at comic. Holdin it is try angle lookin at shape doin think shape cloud shape. It comin out of Stacy Brain brain a cloud. Thinkin: Hmm. Stacy thinkin it lookin at shape. Stacy shakin head.

'It aint it is it.'

Stacy shakin head.

'It is a try angle look.' My pointin at word in comic.

Stacy lookin at try angle. Lookin at plate wrong shape.

Stacy throwin it a way.

Stacy openin lid of box it is big it is on floor under bottom shelf dust. Openin lid. Lookin in box. It is a cake it is big. Stacy put hand it is little it is in cake box in cake. Puttin it in cake. Take a hand out got some on hand. Holdin it at comic doin con pear.

In comic. Lorrence got funny hair shape makin you laugh. Got shape try angle doin hold. Stacy holdin cake shape in hand doin a con pear. It aint even a shape it is. Splodge. Stacy holdin it at comic gettin some on. Stacy doin think it comin out of Stacy Brain brain a cloud it is rainin. Got in it a think thinkin: Hmm.

'It aint even a shape,' I say gettin cross. 'Its cake.'

Me an Stacy look for shape.

On a shelf. It is got. Maths bits an a bobs. It is got. Graph paper plastic toy bits. It is got. Shape.

Stacy holdin shape lookin at shape. It is red see thru plastic a shape.

Stacy got comic. Holdin it at comic. Hold it at hair shape makin you laugh. Holdin it at shape. Lorrence got it in hand.

Stacy got it in hand. Stacy holdin it at shape doin con pear. Stacy doin think in brain. It comin out of brain a cloud. In it got think sayin: Hmm.

'Is it it.'

Stacy noddin.

Me lookin at comic. At shape. At Stacy. At shape.

Stacy lookin at comic. At shape.

'It is it,' I say lookin at it.

Stacy noddin doin smile.

Me doin smile.

Stacy holdin shape. It is. Try angle shape it is red. Stacy doin shake that shape.

'You carnt do it,' I say. 'You have got a get a man do it. A groan up. Or. Not a groan up. Last week. It is a dog did it. Then. Last week. It is. A baby.'

Baby doin shake a rattle. Lorrence got rattle throw it a way. Baby doin cryin. Shake a hand shakin hands wants to do shake a rattle. Lorrence got shape. Give it to baby get it do shake a shape. Baby shakin shape a rattle a shape. Magic comin out of shape. Magic comin out of try angle. It is stars an shapes an colour bits comin out of page. Magic bits turnin page fillin up a page. Lorrence goin in magic. Lorrence in magic havin fun.

Me an Stacy not in magic. Not havin fun. Stacy shakin shape not makin it make magic.

Me tellin her off sayin: 'You carnt do it on purpose. You got a do it by mistake. That is why. That baby.' Me pointin at comic. 'That man. That is why. That is. What it is.'

Stacy noddin.

'It is a only way of doin it.'

Stacy noddin. Shakin shape.

'Stop shakin it.'

Stacy stoppin it shakin it.

214

Me goin out of stock room. 'I am go out of stock room,' I say goin out of sock room.

Me goin out of sock room. Shuttin door.

Stacy in sock room.

Me out of stock room. Lookin at stock room door it is shut. Then.

Me goin in sock room openin stock room door.

Stacy standin in stock room got try angle shape be hind back a sir prize. Stacy lookin at Tom comin in sock room. Stacy in sock room doin think. Thinkin it in brain it fallin out of brain land on floor got broke. Then. Stacy holdin out shape sayin: 'Shake it it aint even magic.'

Me shakin head. It aint workin is it.

Me an Stacy doin trick. Put shape on floor by class room door. It openin Miss Dancer openin door shakin shape.

Me an Stacy sit in seats remain in a seats. Look at that shape pointin at it doin wait. Door openin Miss Dancer open it shakin it by mistake.

But.

Door not openin. Miss Dancer not comin in not shakin shape.

Stacy an me lookin at shape.

Me an Stacy lookin at Stacy an me an Stacy.

Stacy sayin: 'Wheres Miss Dancer.'

Me shruggin.

'Is she got killed aint she.'

Me shakin head.

Me an Stacy doin remain in a seats.

'How long we got a remain in a seats.'

Me shruggin. Not knowin.

'It will be for ever.' Stacy standin sayin: 'We will get

killed.' Stacy sayin it standin up doin walk walkin at door
do open. Lookin out of door. Out of class room door. Out
in corridor.

'Is she there.'

Stacy shakin head. She aint there.

Me standin up. Doin it scared scared of get told off.
Walkin. At door.

Me look out of door. There aint no one there.

Stacy walkin out of door. Not remain in in a seats not
even remain in a class room.

Me walkin out of door.

Stacy holdin hand of Tom got scared.

Me an Stacy out in corridor lookin in class room door in
Behind Class. There is a seats empty there aint a Tom in it
there aint a Stacy in it. There aint a Miss Dancer a teacher.
There is a window blue shinin in it no one out it in play
ground doin play.

Me an Stacy walkin up corridor. Look at notice board.
Miss Dancer lookin at it doin fetch somethin from notice
board. But. She aint there doin fetch. It is got bit of paper
on it got no writin on.

Me an Stacy lookin up corridor. It is got doors it aint got
no one in it.

Stacy let go of hand lookin at door. Openin door.

'It is my class,' I say. 'It is Miss Kinds class.'

Me lookin at door. On it. Where it is got Miss Kind writ.
It aint got Miss Kind writ. It is got writ. Mister Stricter.

'Dont go in it,' I say. 'It is got Mister Stricter in it. He is
gets cross.'

Stacy scared openin door. There is a Mister Stricter in it
doin tell off but. There aint a Mister Stricter.

Me an Stacy in class room. At other end of class room.

It is got a other door a out side door goin out in play ground. It is door what I come in goin a school Prim bringin me in goin in have a word with Miss Kind.

There is my table. Me pointin at table sayin it to Stacy it aint got a crayons.

There is a story carpet got on it a story.

There is Miss Kinds desk got cuddle toys on it but. There aint a cuddle toys. It is Mister Stricter a man.

Stacy openin door of stock sock room. Not got on a socks.

In stock room. It is got in it. O it is Orange Men. Me lookin at Orange Men it is a whole set what you can get a difrent trouser ones all the ones.

Me goin in get a Orange Men.

Stacy stoppin my arm holdin my arm. 'Dont.'

'Orange Men,' I say pointin.

'Dont.' Stacy sayin: 'It is a magic. If you take out a Orange Men. It is gone.'

'What if I jus get one of it.'

Stacy shakin head.

It is a saddest thing in the world. All the Orange Men in the world. You carnt even play with.

Stacy shuttin sock room stock room door shuttin in it a Orange Men a Orange Men prison sayin good bye.

Me an Stacy in class room. There is a tables in it. There aint a children there aint no one in it.

Then. Me find it in pocket. It is in pocket makin shape of it in pocket. It is a sweets a magic sweets a clown. Me pattin pocket shape. Got in it a shape. A shape of it in pocket.

Me an Stacy goin out of class room out out side door. It is hot it is spring near a end. Lookin in class room. Sun flectin on window glass put hand on glass. There aint no one in it. Lookin walkin round a school lookin in school in window at a difrent class room all the ones. Even in a window of office head master bit an can teen bits.

Stacy sayin: 'Where is every one gone.'

Me shruggin.

'It aint even home time.'

Me shruggin.

Stacy shakin head.

Me an Stacy shakin head.

'I wonder.' Stacy says: 'What is. What will happen next.'

Me shruggin. Not even knowin.